Esaias Tegnér

Frithiof's Saga

First American Edition

Esaias Tegnér

Frithiof's Saga
First American Edition

ISBN/EAN: 9783744796606

Printed in Europe, USA, Canada, Australia, Japan

Cover: Foto ©Andreas Hilbeck / pixelio.de

More available books at **www.hansebooks.com**

FRITHIOF'S SAGA

FROM THE SWEDISH OF

ESAIAS TEGNÉR

Bishop of Wexiö

BY THE

REV. WILLIAM LEWERY BLACKLEY, M.A.

First American Edition

EDITED BY

BAYARD TAYLOR

NEW YORK:

LEYPOLDT, HOLT & WILLIAMS.

1871.

PUBLISHERS' NOTICE.

THIS volume is the second of a uniform series of foreign poems lately inaugurated by the publication of "King René's Daughter" from the Danish of Henrik Hertz. It is our intention speedily to add Lessing's "Nathan the Wise," with the splendid introductory essay of Fischer, translated, and edited by the Rev. O. B. Frothingham.

If we are not disappointed in our hopes of the public appreciation of these, we will add others of equal interest. Among those we have in contemplation are Goethe's "Hermann and Dorothea;" Molière's "Tartuffe;" Calderon's "Life is a Dream;" Tasso's "Aminta," translated by Leigh Hunt; "The Wooing of the King's Daughter," from the Norwegian of Muench; "Boris Godounoff," from the Russian of Pouschkine; "Nala and Damajanti," translated from the Sanscrit by Milman; and a translation of Bodenstedt's version of the Turkish songs of Mirza-Schaffy.

CONTENTS.

iv

CONTENTS.

FRITHIOF'S SAGA,

AND ITS AUTHOR.

————◆◆◆————

No poetical work of modern times stands forth so prominently and peculiarly a representative of the literature of a race and language, as the "Frithiof's Saga" of Esaias Tegnér. Swedish poetry, of comparatively recent growth, attained in this work, for the first time, a development in consonance with the character of the Swedish people, and with those qualities of the Swedish tongue which distinguish it from other cognate languages. Purely Scandinavian in its spirit, its scenery, its legendary element, and only indebted to antique culture for a part of its rhythmical form, it combines the freshness and freedom of the early Saga with very high artistic finish and proportion. It appeals at once to the national pride, and the simple human sentiment of the farmer or herdsman, and to the taste of the scholar. Immediately upon the appearance of the poem, its claim to be placed at the head of the imaginative literature of Sweden was recognized. No one attempted to controvert the decision, which has only been strengthened during the forty-three years that have since intervened.

In asserting that Swedish poetry is of recent growth, I refer neither to the old Eddaic literature, nor to those authors of the seventeenth century whose reputation still survives in their native land. Few, indeed, outside of Sweden, have ever read or even heard of the hexameters of Stjernhjelm, or the pious epic of Archbishop Spegel. With Dalin commenced the new era, which nearly corresponds in time to that of England and Germany, and of which Bellmann, Franzén, Wallin and Leopold—names which first carried Swedish poetry to other lands—were the most prominent representatives. When Bellmann died, Tegnér was a boy of thirteen: to Leopold, whom he knew, he dedicated his poem of " Axel," and Geijer and Ling belonged to his own generation. He is thus the central figure of the period—a calm, earnest, beautiful life, in which the fire and enthusiasm of the poet, the sedate strength of the scholar, the tender and solemn humanity of the preacher, and the social and domestic affections of the honest Scandinavian nature, are blended in equal and harmonious measure. Although other of the modern Swedish poets may occasionally surpass Tegnér in depth of reflection, or originality of form, in no one has the poetic faculty attained such a free and plastic grace of expression, while retaining that antique symmetry which always suggests repose.

The secret of this excellence is to be found in the history of his life. Like Linnæus and Thorwaldsen, he sprang directly from the people—from the simple, sturdy, vigorous level of the Scandinavian race. His grandfather was a " *bonde gud* " of the Thorsten Vikingsson stamp : he fought under Charles XII, and after the battle of Friedrickshall, carried his sword and Bible home to his little farm. His wife's name was Ingeborg : whether or not she was beautiful, is not stated. She bore fourteen children to her Frithiof, of whom seven or eight sons inherited plow and sword, and the youngest of all, the Bible. He became a preacher, took a poor country congregation, married the daughter of another preacher, and begat, as his fifth son, Esaias Tegnér, the poet, who was born in the parsonage of Kyrkerud, on the 13th of November, 1782.

When the future poet grew to be an active, impetuous, golden-haired boy of ten, and his oldest brothers, Lars and Elof, were about to enter the University, the father died, leaving only the merest pittance for the family. While the poor widow sorrowed in her cottage behind the birchen avenue of Ingrirud, young Esaias roamed over the country, digging for relics in the old Scandinavian barrows. This youthful vagabondage, however, was not to last long. A friend of his father, the Assessor, Jacob Branting, living near Carlstad, in the province of Wermeland, kindly offered a home to the boy. As the latter wrote a good hand, and was a rapid and correct reckoner, he was installed as a sort of clerk to his patron, whom he accompanied on his official journeys through the province. One who has seen the lovely pastoral scenery of Wermeland: its green, secluded valleys, threaded by the clear, cold streams which sweep down from the distant Dovrefjeld: its superb birch-trees, with their giant white boles, and drooping willowy boughs: its iron forges and foundries, dark forests of fir, rocks of granite and porphyry, glens of primeval wildness, and hills with sea-like glimpses of the Wetter Lake—whoever has seen these, will easily understand how they must have stimulated the boy's fancy, and assisted in the development of his poetic nature. Wandering through Wermeland as a passing stranger, I caught pictures which will never fade from my memory. Even more than on the Sognefjord of Norway, the locality of the original Saga of Frithiof, I recognized the scenery of the poem.

When the boy first began to rhyme, no one knew. He lisped in numbers, and all the occurrences of his life in Wermeland turned themselves into poetry. He became a great devourer of books, often tasking the patience of his kind patron by his complete abstraction and forgetfulness of his duties when he once began to read. He not only turned history and tradition into rhyme, but composed an epic in Alexandrines, on a heroic theme. This habit of mind gave to his poetry, in later years, its remarkable flexibility and grace.

Branting, while sincerely attached to the boy, (whom he had intended to educate for his own position,) soon perceived that the latter's gifts qualified him for a more important sphere of life. He wrote at once to Capt. Löwenhjelm, in whose house Lars Tegnér was tutor, begging that the younger brother might be taken into the family and allowed to study with the Captain's children. His request was granted, and the result showed the wisdom of Branting's course. Esaias learned Latin with wonderful rapidity, attacked Greek with a zeal remarkable in a boy of fourteen, and secretly acquired some knowledge of English from a volume of Ossian. When Lars, a few months afterwards, was offered a more profitable place as teacher, he made it a condition that his brother should be allowed to accompany him.

In 1797, therefore, the brothers took up their abode in the house of the rich iron-master, Myhrmann, in the

mountains, near Filipstad. Lars was tutor, and Esaias
studied in company with the eight sons of the family.
There was a fine library, especially rich in the classics.
Esaias was at once attracted by a folio volume, bound
in parchment—an edition of Homer, printed at Basle, in
1561. With a limited knowledge of the Greek grammar,
he undertook to read the old poet, constructing a system
of interpretation as he advanced. It is stated that in seven
months, so unwearied was his industry, he read the Iliad
thrice, the Odyssey twice, and Horace, Virgil, and Ovid.
At the same time, he was endeavoring to acquire German, English and French, not by means of the ordinary
drudgery, but by boldly commencing with the reading of
the best authors. His progress was so remarkable, that
when Lars gave up his tutorship, he was competent, at
the age of sixteen, to take it in his stead.

A year later he entered the University of Lund,
Myhrmann having generously agreed to share with
Branting the expense of his education. He repaid their
generosity by a devotion to his studies which would
have wrecked a frame unsupplied with the vigorous
farmer-blood of Sweden. He wrote a Latin essay on
Anacreon, received a prize from a literary society in
Gottenburg for an Elegy on his brother Lars, and in
1802, was *primus* of the graduates. During the summer
of this year, he was betrothed, with the consent of her
parents, to Anna Myhrmann, the youngest daughter of
his second patron. The lives of few men exhibit such
evidences of trust and help on the one side, and grateful,
ambitious duty on the other.

Having been appointed teacher and assistant-librarian
at Lund—posts which, if slenderly paid, at least secured
him against want—he had more leisure for his literary

1*

tasks. He was silent, however, for some years. A poem which he sent to the Swedish Academy failed to receive the prize, and this circumstance seems to have either disgusted or depressed him. In other respects, his life was fortunate. In 1806 his success as a teacher enabled him to marry, and in 1810 he received the rank and salary of professor. Shy and reticent as a student, he became self-possessed, brilliant in conversation, genial as a host, and unreservedly tender as a husband and father. The impulse which was to make him the national poet, soon returned with the happy development of his fortunes. The poem of " Svea," sent to the Academy in 1811, not only received the highest prize, but was read and recited all over the land. He was received in Stockholm with great enthusiasm, and while there, published several lyrics which still further increased his popularity. The King appointed him clergyman of two parishes in the neighborhood of Lund, and to this new vocation, although he appears not to have originally desired it, he conscientiously devoted a great portion of his time, visiting his parishioners and assisting them with counsel or active kindness.

For many years, Tegnér's life was uninterruptedly calm and fortunate. In the possession of an ample income, burdened only with congenial duties, happy in his domestic and social relations, and with full leisure for the enjoyment of his literary tastes, the years, as they went by, gave instead of taking away. Each of his poems was caught up gratefully and echoed throughout the nation, on its appearance. In 1814 he published " Nore," written after the conclusion of the Treaty of Kiel : in 1820, " The Children of the Lord's Supper," (of which Mr. Longfellow has made an admirable translation,) and in the following year, the lyrical romance of " Axel." *   About the same time, the last nine chapters of Frithiof's Saga were published, in advance of the complete poem, in a literary periodical called " *Iduna*," and the reception accorded to them determined the immediate publication of the entire work.

The incentive which led Tegnér to seek for the material of his chief poetical essay in the Saga-literature of the North, was undoubtedly given by the Danish poet, Oehlenschläger, whose " Hakon Jarl " appeared as early as 1807.   To the latter is due the credit of being the pioneer in a path leading—as the authors and scholars of that time considered—into a rough, stormy wilderness, peopled with savage and repulsive forms.   The European struggle between the Classic and Romantic, assumed an individual character in Denmark and Sweden.   In spite of Oehlenschläger's success, the prevalent opinion was that the Gothic element was too stubborn, violent and barbarous to be subdued to the service of Poetry. Tegnér's tastes as a scholar might have inclined him to the Classic view, had they not been balanced by his intense national feeling, his early fondness for Northern tradition, and his passionate love for the skies and landscapes of his home.   The publication of Oehlenschläger's " Helge," (I believe in the year 1820,) awoke in him the desire to achieve a permanent triumph in what was still considered a doubtful field.   His patriotism prompted and upheld his genius.

The old Icelandic Saga of *Fridthiofe Fraekna* (Frithiof the Bold), furnished him with a theme most congenial to

---

* This poem has been very correctly and beautifully translated into English by Mrs. George P. Marsh.

his heroic nature. Love, combat, sorrow, storm on the blue billows, trysts in the green grove, exile and longing for the fatherland, guilt and expiation, triumph and crowning peace, were here all offered to his hand. The principal liberties which he has taken with the original story, are in making King Ring die by the "spear-death,"— the runes of Odin, self-carved upon his breast—instead of the "straw-death," and in the rebuilding of Balder's temple by Frithiof, with the reconciliation-scene which follows. Both these changes, however, are in harmony with the spirit of the Sagas. In the first instance Ring heroically completes the recompense he offers to Frithiof; and if, in the second instance, as some critics aver, he has given the poem too modern and sentimental a conclusion, we must not forget that the God against whom Frithiof was guilty of sacrilege was Balder—the *white*, loving, Christ-like deity of the Scandinavian Mythology.

Tegnér, himself, says in a letter to Professor Stephens : "It was never my meaning—though such seems to have been the opinion of many—simply to versify the Saga. The most transient comparison ought to have shown, not only that the whole dénouement is different in the Poem and the Saga, but also that several of the Cantos have a very remote ground in the legend. * * * My object was to present a poetical picture of the old Northern heroic age. It was not Frithiof, as an individual, whom I meant to paint : it was the epoch of which he was chosen as the representative. It is true that I preserved, in this respect, the shell and outline of the tradition, but, at the same time, I thought myself entitled to add or to take away, just as was most convenient for my plan."

Tegnér was certainly right in adding to Frithiof, for

instance, a characteristic which does not appear in the Saga, yet which is an integral part of the Scandinavian nature—that grave, semi-melancholy quality which sets the songs of the land to the minor key, which softens, but never clouds, the blue eyes of its people, which even seems to breathe upon you from the shade of its forests and the dark, forbidding loneliness of its mountain-glens. If, in some respects, Frithiof is slightly modernized, at least he is of pure Norse blood. Whatever has been added to the poem has been taken from kindred sources. Thus the Viking-Code, in Canto XV, is to be found in the *Voluspä*, and a part of Canto II in the *Havamal*. In this respect, the work is consistent throughout. The author must have resisted a strong temptation, when, after bearing the outlawed Viking to the islands of the Grecian Archipelago, he shows the reader, in but a single line, the temples reflected in the tideless wave, and then turns his face again to the North.

In regard to the metrical treatment of the poem, Tegnér says: " The most suitable method seemed to me, to resolve the epic form into free lyric ballads. I had the example of Oehlenschläger, in his ' Helge,' before me, and have since found that it has been followed by others. It carries with it the advantage of enabling me to change the metre in accordance with the contents of every separate song. Thus, for instance, I doubt whether ' Ingeborg's Lament ' (Canto IX) could be given in any language in hexameters, or iambic pentameters, whether rhymed or not. I am well aware that many regard this as opposed to the epic unity, which is, however, so nearly allied to monotony; but I regard such unity as more than sufficiently compensated by the freer room and fresher changes gained by its abandonment.

Just this liberty, however, to be properly employed, requires so much the more thought, understanding, and taste ; for with every separate piece one must endeavor to find the exactly suitable form—a thing not always ready to one's hand in the language. It is for this reason that I have attempted (with greater or less success) to imitate several metres, especially from the poets of antiquity. Thus the pentameter iambic, hyper-catalectic in the third foot (Canto II)—the six-footed iambic (XIV)— the Aristophanic anapests (XV)—the trochaic tetra-meter (XVI)—and the tragic senarius (XXIV)—were scarcely, if at all, heard of in Swedish, previous to my attempts."

Perhaps it would have been better for Tegnér if he had followed " Helge " more closely—varying the metre, as the changes of the theme suggested, without insisting on discovering a separate measure for every canto. Nothing can be more admirable than some of his adaptations, but in other instances the reader feels that something has been sacrificed to the form. Where he has introduced antique metres, as he mentions above, he has been guided by a correct judgment. The lithe limbs of the Swedish language seem to move very naturally and gracefully through these alien dances. But in Cantos III and IV one feels the difficulty of reading a narrative poem by such broken and irregular steps. It was a happy thought to introduce the alliterative Saga measure in " Ring's Drapa." Here the lines move with a solemn and stately freedom which it is quite impossible to reproduce in a translation. The iambic hexameter of the concluding canto is not, as Mr. Blackley asserts in his preface, an " uncouth metre." In the German language it is frequently and successfully employed, and there is no reason why it should not be introduced into English poetry.

I am unable to ascertain the precise time when the first complete edition of " Frithiof's Saga " was published. The second edition, which I possess, bears the imprint of 1825, and Stephens asserts that the first was published the same year. Bishop Franzén, however, in his Life of the poet, says that the popularity which the poem acquired was one of the causes which led to Tegnér's appointment as Bishop of Wexiö, in the year 1824. In the same year he was made Knight Commander of the North Star. Thus evenly and securely had his life advanced, from step to step of success, and at this height rested. Although but forty-two years of age, his productive activity as a poet ceased. Probably the graver duties of his new station, which he fulfilled not only with dignity but with conspicuous success, led him away from the seductions of Song. " Axel " was written during the idle convalescence which followed a severe illness ; " Frithiof's Saga " was the suggestion of a fortunate spirit of emulation ; and, although he planned a new metrical romance, " Gerda," some fragments of which were published, he gave little to the world, from this time, except an occasional lyric.

It is also possible that the change from Lund, with its scholastic atmosphere, fresh, joyous student-life and genial, stimulating society, to the dead quiet and solitude of Wexiö, operated depressingly upon his powers. He could not carry with him the plain room, where his dog Atis, who never neglected one of his lectures on Greek literature, lay at the threshold and warned off all intruders when there were signs of poetry in his master ; nor could the latter take with him the track worn in the floor, where, hour after hour, he slowly paced out his melodious lines. Perhaps, like Campbell, he grew afraid of the shadow which his sudden and undisputed fame cast before him, doubting whether he could surpass his previous productions, and fearing to undo their effect.

The last triumph of his life was in another field than literature. A national Convention of the Clergy was held at Wexiö in the year 1836. Bishop Tegnér presided, and produced, no less by his earnest, noble presence, than by his eloquence, the profoundest impression upon the assembly. In character and influence, at least, he became the acknowledged head of the Swedish Church. In his place in the Legislative Assembly of the kingdom he seems to have been less successful. The heated political discussions in which he was forced to take part troubled his cheerful, serene natural mood, and made him bitter and petulant.

Before this time, symptoms of physical disorder had manifested themselves. In 1833 he was forced to make a journey to the mineral springs of Bohemia, from which he returned without the expected improvement in his health. His bodily condition operated on his mind, and filled him with gloomy forebodings. " God preserve me my reason ! " he wrote at this time ; " there is a streak of insanity in my family. In my case it has manifested itself in poetry, which is a milder form of the disease ; but who knows whether I shall always be exempt from a severer attack ? " Unfortunately, his fears were soon to be justified. An incautious use of the " douche " bath brought on symptoms of apoplexy, after which it was noticed that his mind occasionally wandered. He projected extensive travels, the publication of numerous works, and indulged in other plans of similar character

It was about this time, I believe, that Mr. Longfellow received a letter from him, announcing that a complete edition of his works was shortly to appear, in one hundred volumes! He complained that a wheel of fire seemed to be constantly turning within his brain.

Finally, in 1838 or 1839, he was sent, by the advice of physicians, to the Asylum for the Insane, at Schleswig. Here he soon recovered, returned home, and resumed the labors of his diocese, which he performed until the year 1845. He was then forced to apply for a release: a quiet, phlegmatic condition had supplanted his former nervous excitement, and he gradually grew weaker, both in intellect and in body. Some instinct of his approaching end led him to visit his children and grandchildren at Lund, and afterwards, kneeling beside his faithful wife in the church at Kjellstorp, to receive the Sacrament from the hands of his son. Then he returned home, to hide from the world the slow decay of his faculties. In September, 1846, an attack of paralysis completely prostrated his remaining physical force. He was thenceforth confined to his bed, and utterly helpless, yet his voice regained its former strength and his clouded mind became clear and sound again. As the autumn sun shone into his chamber, he exclaimed: "I lift my hands to the mountains and the dwelling of God!"

At midnight on the 2d of November, while the northern sky glowed with splendid auroral fires, his life gradually ceased, and so gently that the widow kneeling at his bedside could not detect the moment of death. The moonlight, falling upon his face, revealed the peaceful beauty which a pure and happy spirit leaves upon its forsaken clay.

We cannot claim for Tegnér the place which belongs

to a great creative intellect. His genius was essentially lyrical, and it is due to the fortunate circumstances of his life that he stands forth so prominently as a representative poet. Probably no other Swedish poet has so developed and enriched the language; none other has so combined the opposite qualities of freedom and artistic finish. His lines and couplets cling to the memory like those of Byron. There are passages, like the parting of Frithiof and Ingeborg, and Frithiof's Return, which almost every educated Swede knows by heart. I have rarely quoted a line of the poem, while in Sweden, without finding some one to continue the quotation. The author seems to have been unconscious of the undefinable melodious beauty which his poems possess. He was surprised at their great popularity, and on one occasion said: " I had no idea that my poetry would become so *available.*"

The source of his popularity will be found, I think, in three qualities which his poems exhibit: their exquisite melody, their brilliant antithetic passages, and the perfect purity and clearness of their language. " The Swede," says Tegnér himself, " like the Frenchman, prefers in poetry the light, the clear, and the transparent. The profound, indeed, he demands and values also, but it must be a depth that is pellucid. He desires to see the golden sands at the bottom of the wave. Whatever is dark and turbid, so that it does not present him with any distinct image, that he cannot endure." Again, in his " Epilogue," spoken at Lund in 1820, he says :

> " What thou not clearly speak'st, that know'st thou not.
> Twin-born upon the lips are thought and word :
> Obscurely spoken is obscurely thought."

In his collection of epigrams entitled " The Languages,"

although he shows an imperfect knowledge of English by calling it " the speech of stammerers," he thus celebrates the resonant strength of the Swedish tongue :

" Language of honor and conquest, how manly thy accents, and noble !
Ring'st like the smitten steel, and mov'st like the march of the planets."

In *his* hands the praise is hardly exaggerated. It would be difficult to find more perfect examples, both of melody and of imitative harmony, in any modern tongue, than his poems offer. In the wail of the winds and the broken dash of the billows in " Ingeborg's Lament," the shifting hurry and movement of Ellida's struggle with the storm, and the bright, joyous pulsations of spring which beat in the opening of " Frithiof's Temptation," we have an admirable marriage of the thought and the rhythm. Tegnér's gifts, therefore, though not of the highest, were of a very high and rare quality. They illustrate the finest characteristics of his language and race, and cannot perish while either exists.

Tegnér was a man of medium size, slender in his youth, but firm and compact of frame later in life. He had a graceful and symmetrical head, curling blonde hair, fresh complexion, and clear, beautiful brown eyes. His nose was straight and strong, the chin small but well rounded, and a peculiar half-smile played about the corners of his lips. It was a frank, honest, kindly face, sometimes abstracted or overcast with the Northern sadness, but oftener lighted up by the cheerfulness of a nature which rejoiced in its appointed work and attracted to itself the best fortune of life. He was witty and brilliant in society, and many of his remarks and repartees are still in circulation in Sweden. Few poets, in any land, have found the world so kindly disposed towards them, or have left behind them a more serene and pleasant memory.

B. T.

October, 1866.

THE ENGLISH TRANSLATIONS

OF

FRITHIOF'S SAGA.

———◆◆◆———

THE translation of a poem, the charm of which depends equally upon its form and subject, must reproduce the form as nearly as possible. Whether this may be best accomplished by a rigid adherence to the rhythms of the original, or by such variations as the language of the translation suggests, is a question which the translator must solve by his own skill, knowledge, and taste. Frithiof's Saga offers many difficulties in this respect, and of all the English translations which have been published, none will satisfy the Swedish reader.

Mr. Longfellow has given us some parts of the poem so admirably in his article on Tegnér,* that it is to be regretted he did not undertake a complete translation. A poet can only be properly translated by a poet, and none of the English versions which have appeared fulfil this condition. Although the Swedish language resem-

* North American Review, No. CXVI. July, 1837.

bles the English in the simplicity of its structure and in its splendid lyrical qualities, it is richer in feminine rhymes, and abounds with terse idiomatic forms which cannot easily be transferred. Here the Germans, being more nearly related, have succeeded better. The translations of Amalie von Imhof, Mohnicke, and, more recently, Lobedanz, are all tolerably successful reproductions of the original, which, through them, has become completely naturalized in Germany.

The first English translation of Frithiof's Saga was published by the Rev. William Strong, in 1833. This was followed, two years afterwards, by an anonymous attempt, the work of three or four hands. I have not seen the latter, but the oblivion into which it has passed is not indicative of success. In 1838, Mr. R. G. Latham, since distinguished by his ethnological works, published a translation, or rather paraphrase, in London. Even were its execution faultless, the liberties which he has taken with the original would preclude its being adopted as a fair representation of the latter. He not only changes the heroine's name from Ingeborg to Inge-*bore*, but pays so little attention to the Swedish metres that they can only be found in seven out of the twenty-four cantos. He changes hexameter into heroic verse, dactylic into iambic, blank verse into rhyme, with no rule save his own whim.

Here and there Mr. Latham has some very spirited lines, and the whole of " Frithiof at Sea" is faithfully and successfully given. In the " Parting," however, he omits a portion, on the plea that it is " in no degree suited to the English poem "! Moreover, his volume is marred by so many faults of rhyme and metre—points wherein Tegnér is always perfect—that it cannot be read with satisfaction even by one unacquainted with the original.

The translation of Prof. George Stephens (London and Stockholm, 1839), who was a personal friend of the poet, is a very conscientious and laborious work. The measure has been retained, except in the first, second, and last cantos, and the translator's thorough knowledge of Swedish has enabled him carefully to express the author's meaning. But the free, plastic movement of the original is wholly wanting; the English verse is hopelessly stiff and unmusical. Tegnér's liquid-flowing

> "*Liksom en hjelm sin rundel hvälfver*,"

can scarcely be recognized in

> "As Heaven's soft breeze its arched round bends."

This single specimen will sufficiently show that something more is requisite than reproduction of an author's meaning and adherence to his measures, in order to transfer the true spirit and character of a poem into another language.

The translation of the Rev. William L. Blackley (Dublin, 1857) preserves all the original metres, except that masculine are generally substituted for feminine rhymes, and the law of alliteration in Canto XXI ("Ring's Drapa") is disregarded. Mr. Blackley, while condemning the iambic hexameter of the concluding Canto, nevertheless does not venture to change it, like Messrs. Latham and Stephens. Moreover, his verses are much more fluent than those of either of the latter gentlemen, his chief short-coming being that he too frequently gives us rather tame and commonplace English

lines for the poetic fire and sparkle of the Swedish origi-
nals.   Thus, in Canto XII, the beautiful lines :

> " *Och glädtigt skjuter hans svarta svan*
> *Sin silfverfåra på solblank ban,*"

become, in his translation,

> " And gayly his sable swan doth make
> On her glassy course a silvery wake."

A closer adherence to the original text would give us
more of the music—as thus, at a venture :

> " And the joyous speed of his black swan gave
> A silver wake to the sun-bright wave."

So, in the " Inheritance," the terse Homeric picturesque-
ness of " *Springare två gånger tolf, bångstyriga, fjettrade
vindar,*" (steeds twice twelve, impatient, fettered winds,)
is rather weakly given in the line :

> " Twice twelve spirited steeds, like terrible winds in con-
> finement."

This Canto is very well rendered by Mr. Stephens, while
in Mr. Latham's translation it is hardly to be recognized.

As Frithiof's Saga consists, in reality, of twenty-four
ballads, it might be possible to combine selections from
the different translators, and thus obtain a composite version, in some respects superior to any single attempt. On
examining the translations, however, with special refer-
ence to this plan, I found the two former so deficient in
poetic quality, that their occasional vigor would have
scarcely compensated for the break in the smoother flow
of Mr. Blackley's translation. The latter, as a whole, is

greatly the superior, and I prefer, therefore, to present it intact, adding only the few notes which have been suggested by a close comparison with the original.

The notes, explanatory of the old Scandinavian customs and mythological names, follow the poem.

B. T.

ABSTRACT

OF THE

ANCI·ENT FRITHIOF-SAGA.

In Sognefylke, near the holy grove of Balder, dwelt King Bele ; two sons had he, Helge and Halfdan, and moreover a daughter, Ingeborg the Fair.   When he came to die, Bele warned his sons to keep up friendship with the mighty Frithiof, a son of his friend Thorsten, who was the son of Viking.   But the young kings refused scornfully Frithiof's wooing for their sister's hand, and so he vowed revenge, and that he never would come to their assistance.

Soon after, it came to pass that, when King Hring made war against them, they sent to ask aid from Frithiof : he was playing chess, and let himself not be one whit disturbed by their messenger.

Hring conquered, and made the brothers promise Ingeborg's hand to him.

Meanwhile Frithiof had gone to see Ingeborg in Balder's temple (which was a forbidden deed), and there

(xxvi)

he exchanged rings with her; for to him the love of Ingeborg was far weightier matter than the favor of Balder.

To punish him for this contempt of the shrine of Balder, the kings laid upon Frithiof the task of going to the Faroes, and demanding a tribute. So Frithiof, with his foster-brother, set sail in the ship Ellida, the best in all the North; a ship which all said could understand the voice of men. All in the midst of the storm Frithiof spoke of his Ingeborg. At last, when the good ship was near sinking, he hewed Ingeborg's ring in pieces, that his men might not want gold when they went down to Rana's dwelling (she was goddess of the Sea). Afterwards, when they had overcome a pair of storm-sprites, which rode on whales against them, the storm sank down, and they approached the Faroes, where Yarl Angantyr let him take the tribute for friendship's sake, and so he departed.

When he came back, he heard that the kings had burned his dwelling, and that they were just then at the midsummer feast in the grove of Balder. Thither he went, and found few folk within; but Helge's queen sat there, warming the image of the god, anointing it, and rubbing it with cloths.

Frithiof flung the purse with the money in Helge's face, so that his very teeth fell out; and then he was going away, when he beheld the ring he had given to Ingeborg on the arm of Helge's queen. He dragged it from her with such might that she fell upon the ground, Balder's image was thrown into the fire, and the whole temple set in flame. King Helge sought to pursue Frithiof, but his ships had been made useless. Frithiof, just to show his strength, drew such a stroke with Ellida's oars (which were twelve ells long), that they both brake asunder.

Now Frithiof remained an outcast; so he took to the ocean, and he slew the fierce sea-kings, but let the merchants fare in peace. And so, when he had gained great glory and wealth, he hied him back again to the North, and went, disguised as a salt-burner, to the palace of King Hring. Hring knew him, and, pitying his sad tale, commanded that he should be set in the most honorable seat. Queen Ingeborg spake but little with him. Once, when Hring and Ingeborg were driving over the ice, it broke beneath them; Frithiof came with speed and dragged them up again, with sleigh and horse and all. Another day Frithiof and the king went out together into a wood, and the king laid him down to sleep; then Frithiof drew his sword, and threw it away. Then the king told him how that he had known from the first evening who he was. Then Frithiof wished to go away; but Hring gave up Ingeborg to him, and made him, under the title of Earl, the guardian of his heir. Soon after Hring died; then Frithiof married his bride, and remained king. Helge and Halfdan made war against him; but Frithiof slew Helge, and Halfdan had to pay scot to him as his lord.

FRITHIOF'S SAGA.

FRITHIOF'S SAGA.

I.

FRITHIOF AND INGEBORG.

IN Hilding's home together grew
   Two plants beneath his fostering true ;
Two fairer never graced the North,
In youth's green spring-time budding forth.

Strong as the oak, and towering high,
Straight as a tall lance towards the sky,
Its struggling, wind-tost summit blown,
Like helmet-plumes, so grew the one.

The other, like the fragile rose,
When Winter, parting, melts the snows,
And Spring's sweet breath bids flowers arise,
Still in the bud unconscious lies.

(1)

When o'er the earth the storms speed hoarse,
The oak is seen to brave their force ;
When in the sky the spring-sun glows
Open the red lips of the rose :

So grew they glad in childhood free,
And Frithiof was the sapling tree ;
And the sweet valley-rose was there
In Ingeborg, the young and fair.

Saw'st thou the twain by light of day,
In Freya's halls thou'dst seem to stray,
Where wanders many a happy pair,
With rosy wings and golden hair.

But saw'st thou them in moonlit glade,
Dancing beneath the forest shade,
Thou'dst think in airy dance t' have seen
The fairy king and fairy queen.

How light his heart, how glad his thought,
When the first Runes to him were taught !
So proud no king on earth was then,
Since he could teach them her again.

O'er the blue deep he loved to guide
His boat, with Ingborg by his side ;
While she, as sailed they to and fro,
Clapped gleefully her hands of snow.

To gain for her, no wild bird's nest
Too high for him was ever placed ;
Nor even could the eagle strong
Protect from him her eggs or young.

No stream, however fierce its flow,
He feared to carry Ingborg through ;
Sweetly, when 'neath loud falls they passed,
Her little white arms held him fast.

The first fair flower that spring-time bred,
The first wild berry, sweet and red,
The first ripe ear of golden corn,
Faithful and glad, to her were borne.

But all too soon sweet childhood flew,
And Frithiof to manhood grew ;
While to the maid matured, his eye
Beamed full of love's intensity.

Young Frithiof often in the field
Pursued the chase, 'gainst danger steel'd ;
Proud, without either sword or spear,
Unarmed, to slay the grisly bear.

He wrestled with him, breast to breast,
Nor scatheless of his prize possessed,
He carried home the shaggy spoil,
While Ingborg's smiles repaid his toil.

For woman loves a manly deed,
And beauty's praise is valor's meed ;
The one is suited for the other,
As head and helmet matched together.

Then, as the winter evenings sped,
Beside the hearth he sat, and read
Some lay of Odin's halls of light—
Of gods and goddesses so bright.

Then thought he : " Freya's golden hair,
Like a ripe corn-field, waves in air ;
But Ingborg's tresses seem to hold
Lily and rose in net of gold.

" Iduna's bosom, full and fair,
Beats beneath silk, rich, green, and rare ;
But here, 'neath dearer silken folds,
Its place a fairy bosom holds.

" And, like the deep, clear, azure sky,
Beams lovely Frigga's soft blue eye ;
But I know eyes whose gentle ray
Eclipses spring-time's brightest day.

" And shines fair Gerda's cheek alone
Like sparkling snow 'neath northern sun ?
I know of cheeks, whose ruddy glow
A double dawn appears to show.

" A loving heart I know of, too,
　　Like gentle Nanna's, fond and true ;
　　Full worthily, O Balder, we
　　Praise still, in song, her love for thee !

" Gladly in death would I be laid,
　　Lamented by a loving maid,
　　As faithful and as true as she,—
　　Welcome were Hela's home to me."

　　King Bele's child of daring deeds
　　Sate singing, while with busy threads
　　She wove a tapestry of war,
　　With groves, and fields, and waves afar.

　　Upon the snowy woollen field
　　Grew glories of a golden shield ;
　　Blood-red appeared the lances thrown,
　　With silver all the breastplates shone.

　　Still, as she wove it, more and more
　　The hero Frithiof's likeness bore ;
　　When from the frame she raised her head,
　　She blushed with shame, but still was glad.

　　And Frithiof cut, on birch-tree's stem,
　　An I, an F, where'er he came ;
　　And merrily the letters, too,
　　Like their young hearts, together grew.

When riseth up the morning fair,
The king of earth, with golden hair,
And busy life begins to move,
Each on the other thinks with love.

When night with darkness fills the air,
Mother of earth, with raven hair,
And silent stars are all that move,
Each on the other dreams with love.

" O Earth, thou deck'st thyself each year.
With flowers in thy leaf-green hair ;
Give me the sweetest, that may shine
In richest wreath for Frithiof mine ! "

" O Sea, thy gloomy halls possess
Bright pearls in thousands numberless ;
Give me the fairest and most clear,
To weave a chain for Ingborg dear."

" O Peak of Odin's royal throne,
Eye of the world, thou golden Sun,
Did thy bright disc belong to me,
A shield for Frithiof it should be ! "

" O Lamp in Odin's halls of bliss,
Pale Moon, with gentle ray of peace,
Thy fairest beams, if thou wert mine,
To deck my Ingeborg should shine ! "

But Hilding said : " My foster-child,
Check this young fondness, vain and wild ;
Unequal lots forbid the Norne,
And royally is Ingborg born.

" From Odin, in his starry home,
Her ancestors descended come ;
Thou art but Thorsten's son ; forbear,
Since but the great should greatness share."

" My sires lie," Frithiof proudly said,
" In the dark valley of the dead ;
But the falling wood-king left to me,
With his shaggy hide, his ancestry.

" The free-born man, ne'er yieldeth he ;
The world belongeth to the free.
What chance hath lost, may chance repair,
And Hope a royal crown may wear.

" Full nobly born descendeth power
From the great Thrudvang-dwelling Thor :
He heeds not birth, but valor true,
And mightily the sword can sue.

" For my young bride I'll combat now,
Though thundering Thor should be my foe.
Bloom glad, bloom true, my lily fair ;
He who would part us ill shall fare !"

II

KING BELE AND THORSTEN VIKINGSSON.

KING BELE in his palace stood, on his sword
he leaned,
And by him Thorsten Vikingsson, his old, tried friend ;
The comrade who for eighty years his wars did share,
Scarred as a monument was he, and white his hair.

So stand two aged temples, midst mountains high,
Both with age tottering, to ruin nigh ;
Yet words of wisdom still on the walls we see,
And on the roof pictures of antiquity.

" My day is setting fast," King Bele said ;
" Tasteless the mead ; I feel the helmet's weight ;
Dim are my glazing eyes to mortal state,
But Valhall' dawns more near ; I feel my fate.

" So my two sons, with thine, I've called to me ;
Together they're united, as have been we ;

(8)

Once more to warn the young birds am I fain,
Ere from a dead man's tongue all words be vain."

Then to the hall they entered in, as he had willed :
The elder, Helge, whose dark brow with gloom was
     filled ;
His days in temples spent he, with spæmen hoary,
And now from sacrificing came, his hands still gory.

Then came the younger, Halfdan, with flaxen hair ;
His countenance was noble, but soft and fair ;
As if in sport, a heavy falchion bearing,
Like a young maid a warrior's armor wearing.

And last, in azure mantle, came Frithiof tall,
By a full head in stature outmeasuring them all ;
He stood between the brothers as glorious day
Stands between rosy dawning and twilight gray.

" My children," quoth the king, " my day doth
     wane ;
Rule in fraternal peace, in union reign ;
For union, like the ring upon the spear,
Makes strong what, wanting it, were worthless gear.

" Let Vigour be your country's sentinel,
And blooming Peace within securely dwell ;
To shelter, not to harm, your weapons wield,
And let your subjects' bulwark be your shield.
    1*

" An unwise ruler devastates his land ;
  All monarchs' might in people's strength must
        stand ;
  Soon the green splendor of the tree is fled,
  If from the naked rock its roots be fed.

" Four pillars to uphold it, Heaven doth own ;
  Kingdoms are based on one—on Law alone.
  Danger is near where might can sway the
        Ting ;
  Right guards the land, and glorifies the king.

" Helge ! in Disarsal the gods do dwell ;
  But not, like snails, within a narrow shell ;
  Far as the day can shine, or echo sound,
  Far as the thought can flee, the gods are found.

" Oft err the entrails of the offered hawk ;
  False, though deep-cut, is many a Runenbalk ;
  But in the open heart and honest eye
  Odin hath written Runes that ne'er can lie.

" Helge ! be not severe—be firm alone ;
  By bending most the truest sword is known ;
  Mercy adorns a king, as flowers a shield ;
  More than all winter can one spring-day yield.

" A friendless man, however mighty he,
  Fadeth deserted, like a bark-stripped tree ;

With roots refreshed, though fierce the storm-winds
    strive,
By friendship's stream thou may'st securely thrive.

" Boast not thy father's fame—'tis his alone ;
  A bow thou canst not bend is scarce thine own.
  What can a buried glory be to thee ?
  By its own force the river gains the sea.

" Gladness, O Halfdan, doth the wise adorn ;
  But folly, most of all in kings, brings scorn !
  Mix hops with honey, when thou mead wilt brew ;
  Make thy sports sterner, and thy weapon too.

" None is too learned, however wise he be.
  That many knowledge lack, too well know we ;
  Despised the witless sitteth at the feast ;
  The learned hath the ear of every guest.

" To trusty comrade, or to friend in war,
  Be thy way near, although his home be far ;
  Yet let thy foeman's house, where'er it lie,
  Be ever distant, though thou pass it by.

" Thy confidence to many shun to give ;
  Full barns we lock ; the empty, open leave ;
  Choose one in whom to trust—more seek not thou ;
  The world, O Halfdan, knows what three men
    know ! "

After the king rose Thorsten.   Thus spake he :
" Odin alone to seek ill fitteth thee ;
   We've shared each hap, O king, our whole lives
       through,
   And death, I trust, we'll share together too.

" Full many a warning Time hath whispered me,
   Son Frithiof, which I gladly give to thee ;
   As on the tombstones high perch Odin's birds,
   So on the lips of age hang wisdom's words.

" Honor the gods ; for every good and harm
   Cometh from above, like sunshine and like storm ;
   Deep into hearts they see, and many mourn
   A lifelong sorrow for one short hour's scorn.

" Honor the king !   Let one man rule with might ;
   Day hath but one eye, many hath the night.
   Let not the better grudge against the best ;
   The sword must have a hilt to hold it fast.

" High strength is Heaven's gift ; yet little prize
   It brings its owner, if he be not wise ;
   A bear with twelve men's strength can one man
       kill :
   As shield 'gainst sword, set law against thy will.

" The proud are feared by few, hated by all ;
   And insolence, O Frithiof, brings a fall.

Men, mighty once, I've seen on crutches borne,
And fortune changeth like storm-blasted corn.

" Praise not the day before the night arrive ;
  Mead till 'tis drunk, or counsel till it thrive ;
  Youth trusteth soon to many an idle word ;
  Need proves a friend, as battle proves a sword.

" Trust not to one night's ice, to spring-day snow,
  To serpent's slumber, or to maiden's vow ;
  For heart of woman turneth like a wheel,
  And 'neath the snowy breast doth falsehood dwell."

" Thyself must perish, all thou hast must fade ;
  One thing alone on earth is deathless made—
  That is, the dead man's glory ; therefore thou
  Will what is right, and what is noble, do.

So warned the graybeards in the royal hall,
As later warned the Skald in Havamal ;
From mouth to mouth went words of wisdom
    round,
Which, whispered still, through Northland's hills re-
    sound.

Then both full many a hearty memory named
Of their true friendship, in the Northland famed ;
How, faithful unto death, in joy or need,
Like two clasp'd hands, together they had stayed.

" Sons ! back to back our stand we ever made ;
 So ever to each Norne a shield displayed ;
 And now, we aged, to Valhalla haste ;
 Oh ! with our sons may their sires' spirits rest ! "

Much spake the king of Frithiof's valor good,
His hero-might excelling royal blood ;
And Thorsten much of future fame to crown
The Asa sons, who should the Northland own.

" And if ye hold together, ye mighty three,
 Your conqueror the Northland ne'er shall see ;
 For might, by lofty station firmly held,
 Is like the steel rim round a golden shield.

" And my dear daughter—tender rose-bud !—greet
 In tranquil silence bred, as most is meet ;
 Defend her ; let the storm-wind ne'er have power
 To plant upon his crest my late-born flower.

" Helge ! on thee I lay a father's care ;
 Guard, like a daughter dear, my Ingborg fair ;
 Force breaks a noble soul, but mildness leads
 Both man and maid to good and noble deeds.

" Now, children, lay us in two lofty graves
 Down by the sea-shore, near the deep blue waves :
 Their sounds shall to our souls be music sweet,
 Singing our dirge as on the strand they beat.

"When   round   the   hills   the   pale   moonlight   is
      thrown,
And midnight dews fall on the Bauta-stone,
We'll sit, O Thorsten, in our rounded graves,
And speak together o'er the gentle waves.

"And now, ye sons beloved, fare ye well ;
We go to Allfather, in peace to dwell,
As weary rivers long to reach the sea.
With you may Frey and Thor and Odin be ! "

III.

FRITHIOF'S INHERITANCE.

NOW in their graves had been set King Bele
　　and Thorsten the aged,
Where they themselves had desired ; uprose on each
　　side of the deep bay
Mounds high arched, like breasts that the valley of
　　death separated.
Helge and Halfdan together, by old traditional
　　usage,
Ruled in the house of their sire ; but Frithiof shared
　　his with no one,
And as an only son possessed the dwelling at
　　Fraumas.
Three leagues forth was his rule, on three sides round
　　him extended,
Valley and mountain and wood ; and the sea was the
　　fourth of his mearings.
Birch forest crowned the tops of the hills, and where
　　they descended
(16)

Waved fields of rye as tall as a man, and golden-
  eared barley.
Many a fair, smooth lake held a mirror of light to the
  mountains,
Picturing forth the forests, where elks with towering
  antlers
Stalked with the gait of kings, and drank from rivulets countless.
And in the valleys around, far pastured abroad o'er
  the meadows,
Herds with glittering hides, and udders that yearned
  for the milking.
Mingled with these, moved slowly about in flocks
  without number,
Sheep with fleeces of snow, as float in the beautiful
  heavens
Thick, white, feathery clouds at the gentle breathing
  of spring-time.
Twice twelve spirited steeds, like terrible winds in
  confinement,
Pawed in the stalls impatient, and champ'd the growth
  of the meadows ;
Red silk shone in their manes, and their hoofs were
  flashing with steel shoes.

But a house for itself was the banquet hall, fashioned
  in fir-wood ;

Not five hundred, though told ten dozen to every
    hundred,
Filled that chamber so vast, when they gathered for
    Yule-tide carousing.
Through the whole length of the hall shone forth the
    table of oak wood,
Brighter fhan steel, and polished ; the pillars twain
    of the high seat
Stood on each side thereof; two gods deep carved
    out of elm wood :
(Odin with glance of a king, and Frey with the sun
    on his forehead).
Lately betwixt them sat on his bear-skin (this was as
    coal black,
Scarlet red were the jaws, and the paws with silver
    beshodden) :
Thorsten still with his friends, Hospitality sitting with
    Gladness.
Oft, while sped the moon through the sky, the gray-
    beard related
Wonders of far-lying lands, and of many a Vikinga
    voyage
Wide on the eastern sea, o'er the western waves, and
    on Gandvik.
The glance of the listeners silent hung on the lips of
    the speaker—
Hung as a bee from a rose ; the Skald alone thought
    upon Brage,

How, with his silver beard and tongue rune-written,
    he sitteth
Under the leafy grove, and relateth wonders by
    Mimer's
Ever-murmuring stream; himself a living rela-
    tion.
Now in the midst of the rush-strewn hall continual
    flaming
Rose the fire from the mortared hearth; through the
    open chimney,
Heavenly, friend-like stars looked into the banqueting
    chamber.
Round on the wall from hooks of steel were hanging
    in order
Breast-plates and helmets together, while here and
    there from between them
Flashed a sword, like a meteor seen in the dark nights
    of winter.
But more than helmet or sword the shields shone
    bright in the chamber,
Clear as the orb of the sun, or the silvery disc of the
    pale moon.
Then, when a maiden went round the board and filled
    up the mead-horns,
Downwards she cast her eyes, and blushed, and her
    form in the round shields
Blushed like the maiden herself; this gladdened each
    banqueting comrade.

Rich was the house : where'er the eye could turn,
  there did meet it
Cellars and chests well filled, and granaries heaped
  with provisions.
Many a treasure, too, it contained, the booty of warfare :
Golden, with deep-carved Runes, and silver wondrously fashioned.
Three things there were prized above all the rest of
  the riches :
First of the three was the mighty sword, an heir-loom
  ancestral,
Angurvadel, so was it named, and brother of Lightning ;
Far in the east it was forged, as ancient legends related,
Tempered by toil of dwarfs : Björn Blætand the first
  who had borne it.
But Björn paid as a forfeit at once both his life and
  his weapon,
Southward in Groninga-sund, when he fought with
  the powerful Vifell.
Vifell was father to Viking. There dwelt then, feeble
  and aged,
At Ullaröker, a king with an only beautiful daughter.
Lo ! there came from the depths of the woods a giant
  tremendous,

Greater in height than stature of man, and hairy and
    cruel,
Demanding a champion to fight, or else both daughter
    and kingdom.
No man stood forth to strive, nor could find a hard
    enough weapon
His skull of iron to wound, and therefore they named
    him the Iernhös.
Viking alone, who had just filled fifteen winters, with-
    stood him,
Fighting with trust in his arm and Angurvadel, with
    one stroke
Cleft he the terrible foe to the waist, and rescued the
    fair one.
Viking left it to Thorsten, his son, and from Thorsten
    descended
Came it to Frithiof at last. When he drew it, the
    hall was illumined
As by a lightning-flash, or the dazzling gleam of the
    north-lights.
Golden thereof was the hilt; with verses the blade
    of it written,
Wonderful, strange to the north, but known at the
    threshold of sunshine,
Where their fathers had dwelt ere the Asen led them
    up northwards.
Dull was the sheen of the Runes as long as was
    peace in the nation,

But when Hildur began her sport, then glittered they
    blood-red—

Red as the crest of a cock when he fighteth. Lost
    was the foeman

Who ever met that flaming sword in the midst of the
    battle.

Far was that sword renowned, and of swords the first
    in the Northland.

Next in worth to the sword was an arm-ring, far and
    wide famous,

Forged by the Vulcan of Northern story, the halting
    Valunder ;

Three marks was it in weight, of gold unmingled
    y-fashioned ;

On it the heavens were wrought, and the towers of
    the twelve immortals

(Figuring changing months, the Sun's dwellings called
    by the minstrels) :

Alfheim there might be seen, Frey's tower, and the
    sun in new vigor,

As he beginneth to climb the heights of the heaven
    at Yule-tide.

Söquabäck, too, was there ; in its hall sat Odin by
    Saga,

Quaffing the wine from a golden shell,—that shell is
    the ocean,

Colored with gold from the glow of the morn ; and
    Saga is spring-time

Writ upon grassy fields with flowers instead of with
    letters.

Balder appeared there too, as the sun of midsummer,
    glorious,

Shedding abundance around, and shining, the image
    of goodness.

Beaming with light is Goodness, but all that is Evil
    is gloomy.

Weary the sun groweth, mounting so high, and so
    groweth Goodness

Faint on the dizzy height ; so, sighing, sink they to-
    gether

Down to the realms of Hela, the land of shadows and
    darkness.

Glitner was pictured thereon, the palace of peace,
    where Forsete,

Holding the scales in his hand impartial, ruleth the
    autumn.

Many such forms, whereby the progress of light was
    betokened,

High in the vault of the sky and deep in the spirit of
    mortals,

Stood, wrought by master-hand on the ring ; and a
    cluster of rubies

Crowned the circlet fair as the sun doth the arch of
    the heaven.

Heirloom old in the race was the ring ; its origin
    ancient

(Though by the mother's side) reached up to mighty
    Valunder.

Once had the gem been stolen away by plundering
    Sote ;

Widely he cruised through the sea of the North, but
    suddenly vanished.

Rumor at last was borne how on Britain's coast he
    had buried

Himself, with treasure and ships, in a builded sepul-
    chre lofty :

Still there found he no rest, and his grave forever was
    haunting.

Thorsten the rumor heard ; with King Bele he
    mounted his dragon,

Cleft through the foaming waves, and steered his
    course unto Britain.

Wide as a temple-dome, or a lordly palace, deep-
    bedded

Down in the dark green grass and turf, lay the sepul-
    chre rounded ;

Light gleamed out therefrom ; through a chink in the
    ponderous portal

Glanced the comrades in ; pitch-black within stood
    the vessel

Of Sote, with helm and anchor and mast ; and high
    by the tiller

Sat there a terrible form ; he was clad in a fiery
    mantle ;

Moodily glaring sat he, and scrubbed his blood-
spotted weapon

Vainly; the stains remained, and all the wealth he
had stolen

Round in the grave was heaped; the ring on his
arm he was wearing.

"Come," whispered Bele, "let's enter and fight with
this terrible being,

Two men against a fiery fiend." Half angry swore
Thorsten—

"One against one our fathers fought, and alone will I
combat."

Long contended the twain for the right of the peril-
ous conflict,

Which should essay it first; till Bele, taking his
helmet,

Shuffled for each within it a lot, and soon by the
starlight

Thorsten discovered his own; so he smote on the
door with his steel lance.

Open flew bolt and bar; he descended. When any
one asked him

What he had seen in the gloomy pit, he was silent,
and shuddered.

Bele first heard a song, like the spell of witchcraft it
sounded;

Then rose a loud-clashing noise, like the crossing
of weapons it sounded;

2

Lastly, a terrible cry, which was hushed ; then out
    darted Thorsten,
Ghastly, bewildered, disturbed ; with awful Death
    he had battled ;
Bearing, moreover, the ring. "'Twas dear-bought,"
    oft he repeated ;
"Since in my life, save the time that I won it, I ne'er
    was affrighted."
Far was that jewel renowned, and of jewels the first
    in the Northland.
Ship Ellida, the last of the three, of its kind was a
    jewel :
Viking (so say they), as homeward he hied him back
    once from battle,
Coasting the shore, espied a man on a frail spar of
    drift-wood
Carelessly tossing about ; he seemed with the waves
    to be sporting.
Tall, and of powerful form was the man ; his coun-
    tenance noble,
Joyous, but changing, like to the ocean playing in
    sunshine.
Blue was his mantle, belted with gold, with coral
    adornéd ;
Sea-green his hair, yet hoary his beard as the foam
    of the ocean.
Hitherward Viking steered his snake to shelter the
    outcast,

Took him perishing home to his house, and exer-
    cised kindness :
Yet when the host to a chamber would lead him, the
    guest laughed, exclaiming—
" Good are the winds, and my vessel, thou seest, is
    not to be scornéd ;
Fivescore leagues (at least, so I hope), shall I
    traverse ere morning.
Thanks for thy bidding—well 'twas intended ; would
    that some kindness
I, in my turn, could offer, but my wealth lies in the
    ocean ;
Haply to-morrow from me thou may'st find some
    gift by the sea-side."
Next day Viking stood by the sea, and lo ! as an
    osprey
Flieth, quarry-pursuing, a ship sailed into the
    haven ;
No man upon it appeared ; no pilot could be dis-
    covered ;
Yet it steered its winding way through breakers and
    quicksands,
Like as if spirit-possessed ; and when it entered the
    haven,
Reefed were the sails by themselves, untouched by
    hand of a mortal ;
Down sank the anchor itself, and clung with its
    fluke to the bottom.

Dumb stood Viking, and gazed; then sang the glad,
    heaving billows :
" Aegir, protected, forgetteth no debt, and hath sent
    thee this dragon."
Kingly, indeed, was the gift; the bended planking
    of oak-wood,
Not, as in others, joined, was by one growth banded
    together ;
Far spread her lengthy keel ; her crest, like a ser-
    pent of ocean,
High in the bows she reared ; her jaws were flaming
    with red gold.
Sprinkled with yellow on blue was her beam ;
    astern, at the rudder,
Flapped she around her powerful tail, that glittered
    with silver ;
Black were her pinions, bordered with red, and
    when they were bended,
Vied she in speed with the loud-roaring blast, out-
    stripping the eagle.
Saw ye her filled with warriors armed, your eyes
    would have fancied
Then to have seen a fortress at sea, or the tower of
    a great king,
Far was that ship renowned, and of ships the first
    in the Northland

These things, and many more, from his sire did
    Frithiof inherit ;
Scarce in the Northern land was there found an
    heritage richer,
Save with the son of a king ; for the wealth of kings
    is the greatest.
He was no son of a king, yet king-like, in sooth, was
    his spirit ;
Friendly, noble, and mild, with each day growing in
    glory.
Comrades twelve were around him, gray-haired,
    princes in warfare,
Thorsten's steel-breasted knights, with many a scar
    on their foreheads.
Lowest of these on the warriors' bench sate also a
    stripling,
Like to a rose in a withering bower ; Björn was his
    title ;
Gay as a child, but brave as a man, and wise as an
    old man ;
Frithiof's comrade from childhood ; blood they had
    mingled together
(Fosterkin by Northern use), and sworn to continue
Sorrow and joy to share, and avenge the death of
    each other.

Now, 'midst the crowd of comrades and guests who
    had come to the grave-feast,

Frithiof, a sorrowing host, his eyes with tears o'er-
    flowing.

Drank (as our ancestors used) his father's memory,
    hearing

Songs of Skalds resound to his praise,—a thundering
    Drapa,—

Mounted his father's seat, now his, and silently sat
    him

Down betwixt Odin and Frey; that is Thor's place
    up in Valhalla.

IV.

FRITHIOF'S WOOING.

LOUD soundeth the song in Frithiof's hall ;
  The Skalds sing the fame of his ancestors all ;
No joy do they bring
To Frithiof, who heeds not the tales they sing.

Again hath the earth donned her raiment of green,
And vessels swim over the billows again ;
To the shadowy grove
Hieth Frithiof, by moonlight, to dream of his love.

Till lately he joined in the joys of his home,
For Halfdan the merry he'd bidden to come,
And dark Helge, the king,
And with them fair Ingborg persuaded to bring.

He sat by her side, and her white hand he pressed,
And the pressure returned made him happy and blest ;
And he hung in a trance
Of unspeakable love on her favoring glance.

(31)

And often they spake of each happier day,
When the morning dew on their young lives lay,—
Of childhood's hours,
To noble minds a garden of flowers.

They spake of each valley and forest dark,
Of their names deep-carved in the birchen-bark,—
Of each ancient grave,
Where the oaks grew tall in the dust of the brave.

" In the court of the king no such gladness hath smiled,
For Helge is sullen, and Halfdan wild,
And my brothers hear
Nought but flattering song or covetous prayer.

" I have no one " (and here she blushed red as the rose)
" To whom I may speak of my sorrow and woes ;
The court of the king
Far less joy than the valley of Hilding can bring.

" The doves which together we long ago rear'd,
By the hawks' fierce attacks are all scatter'd and scar'd;
One pair alone
Remains, of that last pair take thou one.

" For, doubtless, the bird to his mate will return ;
They even for love and for fondness can yearn ;
'Neath its wing bind for me
One loving word which unnoticed may be."

So whispering sate they the livelong day,
And were whispering still when the sun passed away,
As the evening breeze
Whispers in spring through the linden trees.

But now she is gone, and his joyous mood
Is fled with her presence ; the youthful blood
Mounts to his cheek :
He sighs and grieves, silent, unwilling to speak.

And sadly he wrote of his grief by the dove,
Which joyously sped on his message of love ;
But ah ! to their woe,
From his mate could no more be persuaded to go.

But Björn this mourning could not bear ;
He cried : " What makes our young eagle here
So sad and moody ?
Hath his breast been struck—are his pinions bloody ?

" What will'st thou ?   For here we can fear no need
Of noble food, or of nut-brown mead ;
And the Skalds' long train
Cease not the joyous, tuneful strain.

" His pawing coursers impatient neigh ;
His falcon wildly screams for prey.
In the clouds alone
Will Frithiof chase, by sorrowing o'erthrown.

2*

" Ellida hath no rest upon the wave,
  Early and late at anchor doth she chafe.
  Ellida, be thou still ;
  For strife and warfare is not Frithiof's will."

  At last sets Frithiof his dragon free ;
  The sails swell high, the waves cleaves she ;
  And speedily brings
  Him over the sea to the court of the kings.

  That day were they sitting on Bele's grave,
  And judgment before all the people they gave ;
  Loud Frithiof cried—
  Round hill and vale his voice echoed wide :

" Fair Ingborg, ye monarchs, I love as my life ;
  And your sister I ask of you now for my wife ;
  This union, too,
  Was ever King Bele's purpose true.

" In Hilding's home brought up we were,
  As young trees grow together fair ;
  And our fates above
  Hath Freya woven in gold threads of love.

" No king, no Yarl was my sire, I own ;
  But long shall his name in song live on.
  The fame of our race
  Is witnessed in many a burial-place.

" 'Twere easy for me to win kingdom and land,
But that better I cherish my native strand ;
Where with love I'll watch o'er
The court of the king and the hut of the poor.

" We stand on the grave of great Bele ; he hears
Below us my word, which adjures you with prayers ;
For this boon from you
With Frithiof your buried sire doth sue."

Then rose King Helge, and cried with scorn :
" Our sister was ne'er for a vassal born ;
A king's son alone
Shall Valhalla's beautiful daughter own.

" Go ! style thyself first in the North in thy pride ;
Win maids with thy word, and win men with thy might :
But given to thee,
Our sister, of Odin's blood, never shall be.

" Let the care of the realm be no trouble to thee ;
I can guard it myself, but my serf thou may'st be ;
A place there is still
In our household thou mayest be happy to fill."

" Thy serf," exclaimed Frithiof, " I never shall be !
I'm a man for myself, as my father was, free,
From thy silver sheath fly,
Angurvadel, to fright his security."

Bright flash'd the blue steel 'gainst the sun-lighted
    sky,
And the Runes blazed blood-red as he waved it on
    high :
" Angurvadel," quoth he,
" Thou, at least, art of ancient nobility.

" If the peace of the grave did not pacify me,
    Dark king, my good blade would have brought it to
       thee ;
    Now hear this last word :
    Come never again within reach of my sword ! "

    So spake he, and cleft with a terrible stroke
    The gold shield of Helge, which hung on an oak,
    In twain at a blow,
    And its crash on the grave was reëchoed below.

" Well stricken, good sword ! now lie quiet, and think
    Upon mightier deeds ; but at present let sink
    Thy Runes' bright glow ;
    O'er the blue waves we must homeward go."

V

KING RING.

A ND King Ring from the board his gold seat
thrust forth ;
   Skalds and warriors rise
To list to their monarch's word of worth,
Famed in the North ;
   Good was he as Balder, and as Mimer wise.

Peaceful his land, like groves where gods are found ;
   Never arose
The din of arms within its sheltered bound ;
And all around
   The grass grew green, and sweetly bloom'd the rose.

Justice sate merciful, but undismayed,
   Upon the judging-stone ;
And peace each year abundant tribute paid ;
While widely spread
   In sunshine bright the golden corn-fields shone.

O'er ocean the black-breasted dragons hied
      On snowy pinions ;
Thither from many a distant land they plied,
And from far and wide
      Brought riches more to his rich dominions.

With peace dwelt freedom safely there,
      And though the king
All, as the father of the land, held dear,
Still, without fear,
      Each spoke his mind upon the open Ting.

He'd ruled the Northmen, in peace and right,
      Full thirty years ;
None left his presence unsatisfied ;
And every night
      Sped to Odin his name in his people's prayers.

So King Ring from the board his gold seat thrust forth,
      And all rose glad
To hear the monarch's word of worth,
Famed in the North,
      But, deeply sighing, thus he spake and said :

" In Folkvang sitteth my gentle queen,
      On purple throned ;
But here on her grave the grass grows green,
And flowers are seen
      To bloom by the brook that flows around.

" Ne'er find I a queen so lovely and leal
      My crown to share.
She's fled to Valhalla in joy to dwell ;
But the common weal
      Makes me seek for my children a mother's care.

".With the summer winds often we used to see
      King Bele here :
A lily-sweet daughter he left, and she
My choice shall be,
      With the morning dawn on her cheeks so fair.

" She is young, and young maidens love, I know,
      To pluck flowers of spring.
My bloom is past, and chill winter's snow
Full long ago
      Hath whitened the hoary locks of your king.

" Yet an honest man still her choice may be,
      Though white his hair ;
And if to my motherless children she
A mother will be,
      Then autumn with spring-time his throne may
            share.

" Take gold from my coffers, take bridal array,
      From each oaken chest ;
And follow, ye bards, with your harps on the way,
For meetly may
      He seek Brage's aid who a-wooing doth haste."

Forth with shouting and glee his men
　　With gifts and with gold ;
And the Skalds they followed, a winding throng,
With harp and with song,
　　And the home of King Bele's sons soon they
　　　behold.

Two days they feasted, they feasted three ;
　　When the fourth was come,
To hear what Helge's answer might be
Entreated they,
　　That back again they might hie them home.

To the grove for sacrifice brought he in haste
　　Both falcon and steed ;
Then sought each Vala, and sought each priest,
What fate were best
　　For his sister, the beautiful Ingborg, decreed.

But the omens were evil, though anxiously tried
　　Each Vala and priest ;
And Helge, by evil signs terrified,
" Nay ! " sturdily cried,
　　" For men must yield to the gods' behest."

But merry King Halfdan laughingly cried :
　　" Oh, wasted feast !
Had King Graybeard himself chosen hither to ride,
Full gladly I'd
　　Have helped him myself to climb up on his beast."

The messengers hied them home angrily ;
    To their master's ear
The tale they told, and loud swore he—
" Right speedily
    King Graybeard this stain from his honor shall
        clear."

He smote on his war-shield, which hung at rest
    On a linden tree ;
And his dragons sped over the sea in haste,
With blood-red crest ;
    And the helmet plumes waved merrily.

And to Helge the rumors of war came near.
    In dread quoth he :
" King Ring is mighty—we've cause to fear ;
So in Balder's care,
    In the temple, 'twere better my sister should be."

There sate the loving one mournfully
    In the peaceful shade ;
She wrought in silk, and in gold wrought she ;
Unceasingly
    Her tears fell, like dew on the lily shed.

VI

FRITHIOF PLAYS CHESS.

FRITHIOF sat with Björn the true
   At the chess-board, fair to view ;
Squares of silver decked the frame,
   Interchanged with squares of gold.
Hilding entering, thus he greeted :
" On the upper bench be seated ;
   Drain the horn until my game
   I finish, foster-father bold.

Quoth Hilding : " Hither come I speeding,
For King Bele's sons entreating ;
   Danger daily sounds more near,
   And the people's hope art thou."
" Björn," quoth Frithiof, " now beware ;
Ill thy king doth seem to fare ;
   And pawn may free him from his fear,
   So scruple not to let it go."
(42)

" Court not, Frithiof, kings' displeasure,
  Though with Ring they ill may measure ;
     Yet eagles' young, have wings of power,
      And their force thy strength outvies."
" If, Björn, thou wilt my tower beset,
  Thus easily thy wile I meet ;
     No longer canst thou gain my tower,
      Which back to place of safety hies."

" Ingeborg, in Balder's keeping,
  Passeth all her days in weeping ;
     Thine aid in strife may *she* not claim,
      Fearful maiden, azure-eyed."
" What wouldst thou, Björn ? Assail my queen,
  Which dear from childhood's days hath been—
     The noblest piece in all the game ?
      Her I'll defend, whate'er betide."

" What ! Frithiof, wilt thou not reply ?
  And shall thy foster-father hie
     Unheeded from thy hearth away,
      Because thy game is long to end ? "
Then stood Frithiof up, and laid
  Hilding's hand in his, and said :
     " Already hast thou heard me say
      What answers to their prayers I send.

" Go, let the sons of Bele learn
 That, since my suit they dared to spurn,
  No bond between us shall be tied ;
   Their serf I never shall become."
" Well ! follow on thy proper path ;
 Ill fits it me to chide thy wrath :
  All to some good may Odin guide,"
   Hilding said, and hied him home.

VII.

FRITHIOF'S JOY.

"THOUGH Bele's sons may widely sound,
    From vale to vale, the battle-cry,
I go not forth ; my battle-ground,
    My world, in Balder's grove doth lie.
From thence no backward glance I'll cast
    On kingly spite or earthly care ;
But joys of the immortals taste
    United with my Ingborg fair.

"As long as glowing sunshine hovers
    O'er flowers fair in purple light,
Like rosy-tinted veil that covers
    The bosom of my Ingborg bright,—
So long I wander by the strand,
    By longing ceaselessly devoured,
And, sighing, trace upon the sand
    Her name belovéd, with my sword.

" How slowly pass the hours away !
 Why, son of Delling, lingerest thou ?
Hast thou not marked each isle and bay,
 Each hill and grove, full oft ere now ?
Doth no belov'd one westward dwell
 Who for thy coming long doth grieve,
And flieth to thy breast to tell
 Her love at dawn, her love at eve ?

" But, weary with thy course, at last
 Thou sinkest downwards from the height ;
Her rosy carpet eve doth haste
 To spread for all the gods' delight ;
Of love waves whisper as they flee ;
 Winds whisper love in breathing light ;
Mother of gods ! I welcome thee,
 In bridal pearls arrayed, O Night !

" Each silent star glides through the sky,
 Like lover to his mistress true :
Over the waves, Ellida, fly ;
 Speed, speed us on, ye billows blue !
To home of loving gods we steer,
 Where yonder lies the holy grove ;
And Balder's temple standeth near,
 Where dwells the goddess of my love.

" How happy spring I to the strand !
    Beloved Earth, I press thee glad !
And you, ye little flowers, that stand
    My path to gem with white and red.
Thou Moon, with silvery light that beamest
    Round mound, and grove, and temple tall,
How fair thou sittest there, and dreamest,
    Like Saga in a bridal hall.

" Who taught thee, flowery brook, to tell
    In murmur sweet, my love exprest ?
Who gave thee, Northland's nightingale,
    Those wailings, stolen from my breast ?
The fairies paint in sunset hues
    My Ingeborg on cloud-banks gray ;
A rival beauty Freya views,
    And, jealous, breathes the form away.

" Yet may her image now depart,
    Since, fair as Hope, here cometh she ;
Still, as in childhood, true of heart,
    She bringeth love's reward to me.
Come, darling, to my fond caressing,
    Cling to this heart, where thou art dear ;
My soul's delight, my being's blessing,
    Come to my arms, and linger there.

" As slender as the lily slight,
    As blooming as the opened rose ;
Thou art as pure as Balder bright,
    Yet warm of heart, as Freya glows.
Kiss me, my Ingborg ; let my love
    In joy bring kindred joy to thee ;
For earth beneath and heaven above
    Both vanish when thou kissest me.

" Fear not—no danger cometh near ;
    There standeth Björn with trusty blade,
And men enough, if need there were,
    To shield us 'gainst the world arrayed.
And I, oh ! could I but contend
    For thee, as now embracing me,
Glad to Valhalla should I wend,
    And thou shouldst my Valkyria be.

" Of Balder's wrath what whisperest thou ?
    He, tender god, ne'er loveth ill
Those fond ones who, with plighted vow,
    In loving, his decrees fulfil.
He who true faith in heart doth bear,
    And beaming sunshine on his brow,
Was e'er his love to Nanna dear
    More pure, more warm, than ours is now ?

" There stands his image ; he is near ;
   How softly gazing from above !
And I will offer to him here
   A heart that glows with faithful love.
Kneel down with me ; there cannot be
   For Balder fairer sacrifice
Than faithful hearts, which lovingly
   Unite in truth as firm as his.

" To heaven, more than earth, my love
   Belongs ; despise it, spurn it not ;
For it was born in heaven above,
   And longeth homeward to be brought.
Oh, would we were already sped !
   Oh, would we could together die !
That I triumphantly might lead
   My pallid Ingborg to the sky.

" Then, when to strife the warriors went,
   Through silver portals as they ride,
I'd gaze on thee, a trusty friend,
   And sit rejoicing by thy side.
When Valhall's maidens passed around
   The mead horns, crowned with foam of gold,
To thee alone my pledge should sound,
   Thy name alone with love be told.

3

" On some fair sea-surrounded isle
    I'd build for thee a bower of love,
And there the time away we'd while,
    Midst golden fruits in shadowy grove.
And when, with clear and lovely ray,
    Valhalla's sun illumed the plain,
Back to the gods we'd take our way,
    But long to reach our isle again.

" And I'd adorn with starlight glance
    The golden tresses of thy head,
And high in Vingolf's hall should dance
    My pallid lily rosy red.
Then from the dance my love I'd bring
    To bowers of peace, in fondness true,
And Brage, silver-bearded, sing
    Thy nuptial song, forever new.

" How sings the throstle in the grove !
    Its song is from Valhalla's strand ;
How sweetly shines the moon above !
    It shineth from the spirits' land.
Both song and shining join to tell
    Of worlds of love unmarred by care :
Would in such worlds that I might dwell
    With thee—with thee, my Ingborg fair !

" Nay, weep not—weep not ; life still streams
 Within my veins : oh ! weep no more.
But mortals' love and mortals' dreams
 Are ever upward prone to soar.
Ah ! stretch but hitherward thine arms,
 Bend but thy loving eyes on me,
And see ! how soon thy fondness charms
 Thy dreamer back from heaven to thee."

" Hist ! 'tis tne lark ? "—" Nay, 'tis a dove,
 That cooeth fondness in the shade ;
The lark is slumbering 'neath the grove,
 In sheltered nest beside its mate.
Oh ! happy they, for daylight brings
 To them no cause for dread or fear ;
Their lives are free as are the wings
 That skyward waft the gladsome pair.

" See ! morning dawns."—" Nay, 'tis the glow
 Of watchful beacons eastward shed ;
Our love we still may whisper low,
 Nor yet the happy night is sped.
Belate thee, golden star of day !
 O morning, slumber, slumber still !
For Frithiof may'st thou sleep away
 Till Ragnarök, if such thy will.

" But ah ! in vain the loving hope ;
     Already morning's breezes blow,
Already eastern roses ope,
     As bright as Ingborg's cheek can glow.
The band of wingéd songsters twitters,
     All joyous in the bright'ning sky ;
And earth awakes, and ocean glitters,
     Away must gloom and lovers fly.

" Now mounts the sun in majesty :
     Forgive, O golden god, my prayer ;
I feel thy near divinity :
     How noble art thou, and how fair !
Oh ! that I so my path could tread,
     Like thee, in majesty and might ;
And, proud and glad, my life be clad,
     Like thine, in victory and light.

" Now here, before thine eyes, I set
     The fairest maiden in the North ;
Watch over her, O Balder great !
     Thine image she on grassy earth.
Her soul is spotless as thy ray ;
     Her eye is as thy heaven blue ;
And thy bright gold, that decks the day,
     Glows in her lovely tresses too.

" Farewell, my Ingeborg ! and now
    Another night we must await.
Farewell ! one kiss upon thy brow,
    And one upon thy lips so sweet.
Now sleep and dream of me, and, waking,
    Still on our love in fond thought dwell ;
Count of the hours, as I do, taking ;
    Loving, as I do.   Fare thee well !

VIII.

THE PARTING.

INGEBORG.

ALREADY comes the day, but brings not Frithiof,
    Though yesterday the open Ting was held
At Bele's grave : well chosen was the place
Where Bele's daughter's fate should be decreed.
How many fond entreaties did it cost,—
How many bitter tears,—by Freya told,
To melt the ice of hate round Frithiof's heart,
And win the promise from his haughty lips,
Once more to offer a forgiving hand ?
Ah ! man is stern, and for his own vain pride,
Miscalled his honor, he hath little care—
Ay, less than care—how easily he may
Torture and wound a fondly loving heart.
And hapless woman, clinging to his breast,
Is like the growth of moss, which on the cliff,
Blooming in pallor, difficultly keeps
Its hold unmarked upon the sturdy rock,
Drawing its nurture from the dews of night.

And yesterday my fate hath been decreed !
And over it the evening sun hath set :
Yet Frithiof cometh not.   The pallid stars
Wane one by one, and vanish and depart,
And with each gleam, that slowly fades away,
Some hope within me sinketh to the grave.
Yet, wherefore should I hope ?   Valhalla's powers
Owe me no favor, by myself estranged :
The mighty Balder, in whose shrine I dwell,
I have offended : for no mortal's love
Is pure enough for such a god's beholding ;
And earthly joys should never dare to come
Wherever they, the holy and sublime
Rulers of heaven, have their dwelling made.
And yet, what crime is mine ?   The gentle god
Could ne'er be angry at a maiden's love.
Is it not pure, as Urda's silver wave—
And innocent, as Gefion's morning dream ?
The lofty Sun hath never turned away
Its eye of brightness from a loving pair ;
And starry Night, the widow of the Day,
Amidst her mourning hears their vows with joy.
Can what is holy 'neath the vaulted sky
Become a crime beneath a temple's dome ?
I love my Frithiof, and have ever loved ;
Far as my furthest recollections go,
Growth of my growth, that love hath ever been :
When it began I never knew ; can tell

No hour of life that hath not been of love.
And as the fruit is formed around the core,
And, clinging there, in Nature's time becomes,
Beneath the sunbeams, like a ball of gold,
So have I too grown up, and ripening glad
Around this kernel, all my being is
Only the outward shell that holds my love.
Forgive me, Balder! See, a faithful heart
Into thy halls I brought—with such alone
Will I depart; and speed, with such alone,
Over bright Bifrost's bridge; with such alone
Stand, faithful still, before Valhalla's gods.
There shall my love, a child of heaven, like them,
Mirror itself in shining shields, and fly
On dove-like pinion through the endless space
Of azure heaven to Allfader's breast,
From whence it came. Oh! wherefore darkenest
       thou,
In the gray dawn, thy gentle brow with frowns?
The blood of mighty Odin fills my veins
As well as thine: but oh! not e'en to thee,
Great kinsman, can I sacrifice my love,
Worth more to me than all this boundless heaven.
Yet can I offer all my joy of life,
And cast it from me, even as a queen
Can cast away her royal robe, and still
Remain the queen she was. Well! 'tis decreed
Valhalla's great ones shall not need to blush

For their descendant.   I will meet my fate
As heroes meet with theirs.   Here cometh Frithiof;
How wild—how pale !   All, all is lost—is lost !
With him approacheth, too, my angry Norne.
Be strong my heart !—Oh ! welcome, though how
   late !
Our fate is sealed ; too easily I read
It on thy brow.

FRITHIOF.

Stand there also there
No blood-red Runes, bespeaking scorn and shame,
Insult and ban ?

INGEBORG.

Oh ! Frithiof, calm thyself.
Tell me thy tale : the worst my fears foretold
Full long ago.   For all am I prepared.

FRITHIOF.

I reached the Ting, where stand our fathers' tombs,
And round its grassy sides, shield crowning shield,
And sword in hand, the Northland's sons arrayed,
One ring within another gathered, stood
Up to the summit ; on the judging-stone,
Like a dark thunder-cloud, King Helge sate,—
The pallid sacrificer, with forbidding looks ;
And by him, thoughtless, leaning on his sword,
A fair, well-fashioned youth, King Halfdan sate.
 3*

Then stood I forth, and cried : " War cometh near ;
The foemen's shields upon our borders clash.
King Helge, peril threateneth thy realm.
Give me thy sister, and I bring to thee
This arm to combat, which may service do,
And let our former quarrel be forgot.
With Ingborg's kindred love I not to strive.
Bethink thee, monarch, and together save
Thy golden crown, thy sister's happiness.
Here is my hand ; by Thor divine, no more
Than this last time I offer it for peace."
A shout filled all the Ting, a thousand swords
Clashed loud approval on a thousand shields.
Far fled the sounds into the lofty skies,
Which drank the shouts of freemen for the right :
" Oh ! give him Ingeborg, the gentle lily ;
No fairer ever in our valleys bloomed :
His is the bravest sword in all the land.
Oh ! give him Ingeborg." Our foster-father,
The aged Hilding, with the silvery beard,
Stood forth, and spake, in words of wisdom deep,
Short, pithy pleas, which rang like strokes of
    swords.
And Halfdan, rising from the royal seat,
Himself besought, with many a word and sign.
All was in vain, and bootless every prayer
So beaming sunshine, on the barren rock,
No fruit enticeth from its stony heart ;

And Helge's dark, unchanging visage spake
To all entreaties still a ghastly Nay.
" A yeoman's son," said he, at length, in scorn,
" Might wed with Ingborg; but to Valhall's daughter
Becometh ill a sacrilegious mate.
Hast thou not, Frithiof, broken Balder's peace?
Hast thou not seen my sister in his shrine,
When Day had hid itself before the crime?
Answer me, Yea, or Nay!"   Loud rose a cry
Amidst the crowd of men: " Say Nay—say only
      Nay,
Thou Thorsten's mighty son, almost a king;
Thy word we trust, and we for thee will sue;
Only say Nay, and Ingeborg is thine."
" My joy of life hangs on a single word,"
I said; " yet fear not therefore thou, O King!
I would not lie for all Valhalla's bliss,
Then scarce for earthly joy: I saw thy sister,
And spake with her at night-time in the temple;
Yet thus I never broke the peace of Balder."   Here
I had to cease.   A scream of horrid fear
Spread through the Ting; those who beside me stood
Fell off as from a plague-besmitten man.
Where'er I looked, their superstitious fear
Had hushed each tongue, and every face was pale,
Which just before had flushed with joyous hope.
There conquered Helge : then, in ghastly tones,
Hollow and deep (like those of Vala dread,

In Vegtamsquida, when to Odin singing
Of Hela's triumph, and the Asen's fall),
Thus spake he gloomy : " Banishment or death
I might denounce by our ancestral laws
Against thy sin ; but I will show me mild
As Balder is, whose-holiness thou'st slighted.
In western ocean doth a cluster lie
Of islands, where Jarl Angantyr bears sway :
A stated yearly tribute paid the Jarl
While Bele lived, but never since his death.
Cross thou the sea, and fetch that tribute back,
So may thy service for thy sin atone."
Then in mean scorn he added : " Hard of hand,
They say, he is ; and, like the dragon Fafner,
He watcheth o'er his gold ; but who can stand
Against our second Sigurd, Fafner's bane ?
This shall a worthier adventure prove
Than maidens to beguile in Balder's grove.
Next summer let us see thee homeward wend
With all thy glory, and thy treasure too :
Else shalt thou be a knave in Northmen's eyes ;
And all thy lifetime peaceless in the land."
Such was his speech ; and so the Ting dispersed.

INGEBORG.

And now thy purpose ?

FRITHIOF.

Have I aught to choose ?

Hangeth my honor not on his demand ?
And I must free it—ay, if Angantyr
His wretched gold in Nastrand's waves should hide.
This day shall I depart.

INGEBORG.

And leavest me ?

FRITHIOF.

Nay, nay, I leave thee not ; thou, too, shalt come.

INGEBORG.

Impossible !

FRITHIOF.

O Ingborg, hear me first.
Thy crafty brother seemeth to forget
That Angantyr hath been my father's friend,
As well as Bele's ; and he yet may give
With good will what I ask : should he refuse,
I have a sharp-tongued, mighty advocate
My cause to plead ; it hangeth by my side.
The gold he loves to Helge I will send,
Freeing forever, thus, myself and thee
From service to this crownéd hypocrite.
But we ourselves, my Ingborg fair, will spread
Ellida's sails ; and over seas unknown
She'll bear us bounding to a happier land,
And find sweet shelter for our banished love.

What care have I for Northland—for a race
Who, when their priests but speak, in fear grow pale,
And rude would tear the flow'r-crowned cup of life
From out the sanctuary of my heart?
By Freya, nay, they never shall succeed!
None but a slave will to his mother-soil
Be chained unwilling; I will wander free,
Free as the mountain winds.   A little clay
Gathered from Bele's and my father's graves
Finds place upon our bark; and that is all
That we of Fatherland can ever need.
O my beloved, warmer sunshine glows
Than our pale light above the snowy hills;
And we can find a fairer heaven than here,
Where gentle stars with god-like beam glance down,
And in the happy, balmy summer night
Watch in the laurel-groves each loving pair.
Full far my father, Thorsten, Viking's son,
Wandered in warfare; and full oft he told
By blazing hearth, through the long winter nights,
Of southern ocean, with its islands fair:
Green groves reflected in the shining waves.
In days of old ruled there a mighty race;
And gods tremendous in their marble shrines:
But now forsaken stand they.   Grass grows o'er
The mounds deserted; and wild flowers hide
Inscriptions which the old world's wisdom show.
Ruins of tapering pillows there grow green,

Covered with leaves of clinging southern weeds,
And all around the lovely earth brings forth
Harvests unsown of all that men can need.
And golden fruits on shadowy branches glow :
There grapes in heavy clusters on the vine
Hang purple-red, and ripe as thy sweet lips :—
There, Ingeborg, we'll found beyond the waves
Another Northland, fairer far than here ;
And with our faithful love rejoice once more
Deserted shrines and temples, and delight
With mortal fondness the forgotten gods.
Then if some mariner with flapping sail
(For there no storms engage) drift past our isle
By rosy sunset, and with joyous gaze
Look from the ruddy ocean to the strand,
Then on the temple's threshold shall he see
Thee, a new Freya (her, methinks, they name
In their tongue Aphrodite)—shall behold
Thy golden locks light floating in the breeze ;
Thine eyes more radiant than the southern sky.
And growing round thee, coming by degrees,
A temple-dwelling little Alfen-race
With flushing cheeks, as if the South had set
All its fair roses in the northern snows.
Ah ! Ingeborg, how fair, how near doth stand
Each earthly joy to two fond, loving hearts !
If boldly grasped whene'er its time be come,
It follows willingly, and builds for them

A Vingolf even here on earth below.
Come, hasten ! even now each word we speak
Stealeth away an instant from our joy.
All is prepared, and, eager for her flight,
Ellida flaps her darkling eagle-wings,
And the fresh-breathing north wind calls us forth
For ever from this superstitious shore.
How ?   Lingerest thou ?

INGEBORG.

Alas ! I cannot follow thee.

FRITHIOF.

Not follow me ?

INGEBORG.

Ah ! Frithiof, thou art happy !
Following no man, thou canst forward go,
Like thy swift vessel ; at the rudder stands
Thy will alone ; and so thou steerest forth,
With steady hand, above the angry waves.
Alas ! how different my lot must be !
My destiny in other hands must lie,
Which yield not up their prey, although it bleed.
Self-sacrifice, and grief, and pining is
The freedom of the daughter of a king.

FRITHIOF.

Art thou not free, whene'er thou wilt?—sitteth thy sire
Not in his grave?

INGEBORG.

      Ah! Helge is my father,
Or standeth in his place; without his will
I cannot wed: and Bele's daughter steals
No happiness, however near it lie.
For what were woman, thus self-willed, to break
Those bonds wherewith the wise Allfader linketh
Ever the weaker being to the strong?
In the pale water-lily is her type,
Sinking or rising on the changing waves;
Above it speeds the sailor's keel away,
And recks not how it wound the tender stem:
Such is its destiny; and yet, as long
As clings the root tenacious in the sand,
It sprouteth ever forth; its pallid hues
It borroweth from sister-stars above,
Itself a star upon the azure deep:
But, by the roots uptorn, it drifts away,
A faded leaf upon the desert wave.
Last night—and oh! a wretched night it was—
Anxious as watch'd I, and thou camest not,
Thoughts all-terrific, offspring of the night,
The raven-locked, passed constantly before
My waking eyes, which burned, but could not weep,

Balder himself, the bloodless god, did seem
To bend upon me glances filled with rage.
And so, last night, I have revolved my fate,
And thus determined : I will linger here,
Submissive victim to my brother's will.
Yet it is well that then I had not heard
Thy hope-breathed dreams of cloud-imagined isles,
Where ever glows the heavenly sunset's light
O'er flow'ry lands of tranquil peace and love.
How few can tell how weak we are ; the dreams
Of childhood, long-forgotten, rise anew
And whisper in my ear with gentle tones
As well remembered as a sister's voice,—
As sweet and tender as a lover's tones.
But now I will not hearken, will not heed
Those sweet, persuading, once beloved words !
Can I, the Northland's child, there southwards dwell ?
I am too pale for southern roses' bloom :
Too colorless my thought for Southland's glow.
It would be melted 'neath its burning sun ;
And longingly my weary eye would strain
Towards the bright north-star, which unchanging
          keeps
Its heavenly watch above our fathers' graves.
My noble Frithiof shall not fly away
From the dear fatherland he should defend,
Nor ever cast his wide-spread fame aside
For such a trifle as a maiden's love.

A life in which the sun spins year by year,
Each day unvarying from the day before,
A sameness beautiful, but everlasting,
May suit for maidens ; but for manly souls
Like thine a tranquil life is wearisome.
Thou thrivest best when storms tumultuous ride
Their foaming battle-steeds across the seas,
And on a swaying plank, for life or death
Battlest with peril for the meed of fame.
The lovely desert thou hast painted were
A grave untimely for thine unborn deeds ;
Together with thy shield, thy free-born soul
Would gather rust.   Oh ! that shall never be :
Ne'er will I steal away my Frithiof's name
From Skalden songs, and never will I quench
My hero's glory in its rosy dawn.
Be wise, my Frithiof; let us yield before
The mighty Nornes, and, so submitting, save
At least our honor from the wreck of fate ;
Our joy of life we can no longer save.
So we must separate.

FRITHIOF.

But wherefore so—
Because a sleepless night thy mind disturbs ?

INGEBORG.

Because thy safety and my worth demand.

FRITHIOF.

A woman's worth in manly love is found.

INGEBORG.

He loves not long who doth not honor too.

FRITHIOF.

Inconstant stubbornness no honor wins.

INGEBORG.

A noble stubbornness is love of right.

FRITHIOF.

But yesterday it strove not with our love.

INGEBORG.

Nor doth to-day, but with our flight the more.

FRITHIOF.

It is necessity that calls us.   Come !

INGEBORG.

Needful alone is what is right and noble.

FRITHIOF.

High mounts the sun, the time is fleeting by.

INGEBORG.

Ah me ! it is gone by—gone by for ever.

FRITHIOF.

Bethink thee well,—is this thy last resolve ?

INGEBORG.

I have bethought me well, and so resolve.

FRITHIOF.

Farewell, then, Helge's sister—fare thee well !

INGEBORG.

O Frithiof, Frithiof, is it thus we sever ?
And hast thou, then, no kindly glance for me,
Thy childhood's friend ; hast thou no hand to offer
To her unhappy, whom thou once didst love ?
Think'st thou I stand on roses here, and cast
Away with senseless smile my lifetime's joy,
Uprooting from my heart without a pang,
The hope belov'd which with my growth hath grown ?
Hast thou not been the day-dream of my heart ?
All that I ever knew of joy was Frithiof ;
And all that life hath generous or brave
Forever in my mind thy image took.
Oh ! shadow not that image to me ; meet
With harshness not the poor weak girl, who offers
All that on earth's wide circuit she holds dear,—
All that can dearest be in Valhall's halls.
Frithiof, this sacrifice is hard enough,
A word of comfort it might well deserve.

I know thou lovest me ; I knew it well,
Already when our days began to bloom,
And surely shall thy Ingborg's love pursue
Thee many a year, where'er thou mayest wend.
But din of arms at length will dull thy grief,
Which, floating far upon the stormy waves,
Will find no place beside thee on the bench,
When, glad with victory, thou drain'st the horn.
Yet now and then, when in the peace of night
Thou musterest memories of the bygone days,
Amongst them may flit by an image pale
Well known to thee, and bringing greeting fond
Of thy dear home, and it shall bear the form
Of the pale maid who dwells in Balder's grove.
Thou wilt not drive it from thee, though its glancc
May troubled seem ; ah ! whisper but a word,
One word of friendship to it, and the winds
Of night on faithful wings will waft it me ;
One comfort left, the only one I own :
For I have nothing to disperse my grief ;
All that surroundeth me recalleth it :
These lofty temple halls but speak of thee ;
Even Balder's image in the still moonlight,
Threatening no longer, seems thy form to take.
Seaward I look,—there swam thy keel, and clave
Its way to me awaiting on the strand.
Landward I look,—there standeth many a stem
With Ingborg's name deep carved upon the bark :

The trees stretch out, and so the name grows faint,
'Tis but a token, as they say, of death.
I ask of daylight, when it saw thee last?
Of night I ask, but she remaineth still.
Even the sea, which beareth thee, returneth
My questions only with a sigh to shore.
Greetings I'll send thee in the sunset red,
Quenching its fires afar amongst thy waves.
Each cloud-ship that sails through the sky shall bear
A freight of sorrow from the lonely one.
So in the maiden's chamber will I sit,
A dark-clad widow, mourning for her joy;
Embroidering broken lilies in the frame,
Till Spring a newly-woven carpet spread,
Covered with sweeter lilies, o'er my grave;
Or, taking up my harp, my endless woe
Breathe forth in deepest tones of misery,
Or burst in tears, as now.

FRITHIOF.

Thou conquerest, child of Bele; weep no more;
Forgive my anger: ah! 'twas nought but grief,
Which for a moment borrowed anger's garb,—
A garb which I can never carry long.
Oh! Ingeborg, thou art my Norna good;
The noble best nobility can teach;
The wisdom of necessity can have
Never a better advocate than thee,

Oh! lovely Vala, with the rosy lips.
Yes, I will yield before necessity,—
Will part from thee, but never part from hope.
Hope I'll bear with me o'er the western waves,
I'll bear it with me to the gates of death.
With the first spring-day will I hie me home ;
Me shall King Helge soon, I trust, behold,
My vow accomplished, and my task fulfilled,
The crime forgiven of which I stand accused.
Then shall I ask thee—nay, shall claim thy hand
Upon the open Ting, 'midst naked swords,
From Helge not, but from the Northland race,
That is thy sponsor true, thou child of kings.
I have a word for him who shall refuse.
Till then, farewell—be true, remember me ;
And take, in memory of our childhood's love,
My arm-ring here, Valunder's beauteous work,
With heavenly wonders graven on the gold ;
Still worthier wonder is a faithful heart.
How well it clingeth to thy dazzling arm—
A glow-worm glittering on a lily-stem.
Farewell, my bride, my darling—fare thee well !
Bide a few moons, and all our grief is changed.

                       (*He goes.*)

INGEBORG.

How proud, how valiant, and how strong in hope !
The point he setteth of his trusty sword

At Norna's breast, and crieth, " Thou must yield ! "
Alas ! my poor Frithiof, Norna never yields ;
She goes her way, and laughs at Angurvadel.
How little knowest thou my sullen brother !
Thine open, valiant soul can never fathom
The gloomy depths of his ; nor tell the hate
That burneth fiercely in his envious breast.
His sister's hand to thee he'll never give.
Far sooner will he risk his crown, his life,
And offer me to hoary Odin, or
To agéd Ring, with whom he now contends.
Where'er I look, I see no hope for me ;
Yet am I glad, it liveth in thine heart.
So I will keep my sorrow for myself,
And, oh ! may all the good gods follow thee !
Thine arm-ring here shall help me well to tell
The dreary months off, in consuming care ;
Two, four, and six,—then mayest thou return.
But never find again thine Ingeborg.

4

IX.

INGEBORG'S LAMENTATION.

" AUTUMN is here ;
   High-heaving Ocean its waves doth rear ;
And still, here, far from my home,
Gladly I'd roam.

" Long did I view
   His sail in the west, on its course as it flew ;
Oh ! happy, my Frithiof to follow
Over the billow.

" Ye blue billows rough,
   Swell not so high ; ye speed swiftly enough.
Shine brightly, ye stars, to display
To my Frithiof his way.

" He will be home
   With Spring ; but his dear one will come
No more to his love-breathing call
In valley or hall.

(74)

" Ghastly, and cold
  To the voice of his love, she shall lie in the
        mould ;
  Or, offered for her brother's need,
  Lamenting, bleed.

" Thou, his falcon, art left ;
  Mine shalt thou be, and I'll treasure the gift ;
  But by me, thou wing'd hunter of heaven,
  Thy food shall be given.

" Thy place thou shalt claim,
  Displayed on his wrist on the 'broidering frame ;
  Thy wings of silver folding,
  Thy talons golden.

" Freya, in need,
  Took falcon's wings once, through creation to
        speed,
  And her Oedur belovéd sought forth
  In south and in north.

" E'en couldest thou share
  Thy pinions with me, scarce my weight could they
        bear :
  'Tis death, and death only, that brings
  Celestial wings.

" Sky-hunter brave,
  Perch on my shoulder, and gaze o'er the wave.
  Alas ! how long may we gaze
  While Frithiof delays.

" When I am dead,
  He will return ; to my message give heed—
  Welcome and comfort, over and over,
  My sorrowing lover."

X.

FRITHIOF AT SEA.

NOW, King Helge stood
    In fury on the strand,
And in embittered mood
    Adjured the Storm-fiend's band.

Gloomy is the heaven growing,
    Through desert skies the thunders roar,
In the deep the billows brewing
    Cream with foam the surface o'er.
Lightnings cleave the storm-cloud, seeming
    Blood-red gashes in its side ;
And all the sea-birds, wildly screaming,
    Fly the terrors of the tide.

    " Storm is coming, comrades ;
      Its angry wings I hear
      Flapping in the distance,
      But fearless we may be.

Sit tranquil in the grove,
And fondly think on me,
Lovely in thy sorrow,
Beauteous Ingeborg."

———

Now two storm-fiends came
Against Ellida's side ;
One was wind-cold Ham,
One was snowy Heyd.

Loose set they the tempest's pinions,
Down diving in ocean deep,
Billows, from unseen dominions,
To the god's abode they sweep.
All the powers of frightful death,
Astride upon the rapid wave,
Rise from the foaming depths beneath,
The bottomless, unfathomed grave.

" Fairer was our journey
Beneath the shining moon,
Over the mirrory ocean,
To Balder's sacred grove.
Warmer far than here
Was Ingborg's loving heart ;
Whiter than the sea-foam
Heaved her gentle breast."

———

Now Solundar-oe
  Ariseth from the foam ;
Calmer the sea doth grow
  As near the port they come.

But for safety valiant Viking
  Will not readily delay ;
At the helm he stands, delighting
  In the tempest's stormy play.
Now the sheets more close belaying,
  Swifter through the surge he cleaves ;
Westward, further westward flying
  Lightly o'er the rapid waves.

  " Yet longer do I find it sweet
      To battle with the breeze,
    Thunderstorm and Northman meet,
      Exulting on the seas.
    For shame might Ingborg blush,
    If her osprey flew,
    Frightened by a storm-stroke,
    Heavy-winged to land."

Now ocean fierce battles ;
  The wave-troughs deeper grow,
The whistling cordage rattles,
  The planks creak loud below.

But though higher waves appearing
   Seem like mountains to engage,
Brave Ellida, never fearing,
   Mocks the angry ocean's rage.
Like a meteor, flashing brightness,
   Darts she forth, with dauntless breast,
Bounding, with a roebuck's lightness,
   Over trough and over crest.

   " Sweeter were the kisses
     Of Ingborg, in the grove,
     Than here to taste in tempest
     High-sprinkled, briny foam.
     Better the royal daughter
     Of Bele to embrace,
     Than here, in anxious labor,
     The tiller fast to hold."

———

   Whirling cold and fast,
     Snow-wreaths fill the sail ·
   Over deck and mast
     Patters heavy hail.

The very stem they see no more,
   So thick is darkness spread ;
As gloom and horror hover o'er
   The chamber of the dead.

Still to sink the sailor dashes
   Implacable each angry wave ;
Gray, as if bestrewn with ashes,
   Yawns the endless, awful grave.

   " For us, in bed of ocean,
      Azure pillows Ran prepares ;
      On thy pillow, Ingeborg,
      Thou thinkest upon me.
      Higher ply, my comrades,
      Ellida's sturdy oars ;
      Good ship, heaven-fashioned,
      Bear us on an hour."

   O'er the side apace
      Now a sea hath leapt :
   In an instant's space
      Clear the deck is swept.

From his arm now Frithiof hastens
   To draw his ring, three marks in weight ;
Like the morning sun it glistens,
   The golden gift of Bele great.
With his sword in pieces cutting
   The famous work of pigmies' art,
Shares he quickly, none forgetting,
   Unto every man a part.
   4*

" Gold is good possession
   When one goes a-wooing ;
   Let none go empty-handed
   Down to azure Ran.
   Icy are her kisses,
   Fickle her embraces ;
   But we'll charm the sea-bride
   With our ruddy gold."

———

Fiercer than at first,
    Again the storm attacks,
And the sails are burst,
    And the rudder cracks.

O'er the ship half buried tearing,
   Now the waves an entrance gain ;
At the pumps the crew, despairing,
   Fail to drive them forth again.
Frithiof now no longer doubteth
   That he Death hath got on board,
Still above the storm he shouteth,
   Dauntless, with commanding word.

" Björn, come to the rudder ;
   Hold it tight as bear's hug ;
   Valhall's power sendeth
   No such storm as this.

Now at work is magic :
Coward Helge singeth
Spells above the ocean :
I will mount to see."

———

Like as martins fly,
   Sped he up the mast,
And thence, seated high,
   A glance around he cast.

A whale before Ellida gliding,
   Like a loose island, seeth he,
And two base ocean demons riding,
   Upon his back, the stormy sea.
Heyd, in snow-garb shining brightly,
   In semblance of an icy bear ;
Ham, his loud wings flapping widely,
   Like a storm-bird high in air.

   " Now, Ellida, let us see
     If in truth thou bearest
     Valor in thine iron-fastened
     Breast of bended oak.
     Hearken to my calling,
     If thou be heaven's daughter :
     Up ! and with thy keel of copper
     Sting this magic whale."

Now heed Ellida giveth
    Unto her lord's behest :
With a bound she cleaveth
    Deep the monster's breast.

Forth a stream of blood hath bounded,
    Spouting upwards to the sky,
Diving down, the brute, deep-wounded,
    Sinketh, bellowing, to die.
Together now two darts are cast,
    Flung by Frithiof's arm so fierce ;
Through the ice-bear one hath passed,
    One the storm-bird's breast doth pierce. .

" Well stricken, brave Ellida !
    Not soon again, I wager,
    Shall Helge's magic vessel
    Rise on the gory wave.
    Heyd and Ham no longer
    Now bewitch the ocean ;
    Full bitter is the biting
    Of the purple steel."

At once the storm-wind, leaving
    The ocean calm and clear,
Still wafteth on its heaving
    The ship to islands near.

And, all at once, the sun appearing,
  Like a monarch in his hall,
New life and new delights seems bearing
  To ship and wave, to hill and vale ;
His silent radiance crowneth high
  The lofty cliff, the forest's bound :
And all rejoicingly descry
  The grassy shores of Efjesund.

  " Pale Ingeborg's entreaties
    Have risen to Valhalla,—
  Her knees my lily bended
    Before the golden shrine.
  The tears in her eyes so lovely,
  The sighs of her swan-like bosom,
  Have touched the hearts of immortals :
  Now let us give them thanks."

  ———

  But Ellida's prow
    Hath stricken with such force,
  That slow she crawleth now,
    A-weary of her course.

Weary, too, with dangerous sailing
  Now are Frithiof's comrades bold,
E'en the swords they lean on, failing
  Feeble forms erect to hold.

On sturdy shoulders Björn doth ferry
   Four from Ellida to the land ;
But mighty Frithiof eight doth carry
   Down to the fire upon the strand.

   " Blush not, pale companions,
     Waves are sturdy Vikings,
     And bitter 'tis to battle
     With the ocean maids.
     See, the mead-horn cometh,
     On feet of gold it circleth ;
     Our limbs benumbed we'll warm again
     With skoal for Ingeborg."

XI.

FRITHIOF WITH ANGANTYR.

NOW also ye the tale shall hear
    How, with his vassals all,
Drank joyfully Yarl Angantyr,
    In the fir-wood fashioned hall.
In mirth and gladness sitting, he
    The blue waves looked upon,
As down the sun sank in the sea,
    Like to a golden swan.

In the deep bow of the window wide
    Old Halvar, keeping ward,
With one eye viewed the spreading tide,
    With one his mead did guard.
A habit strange the old man had—
    He'd ever empty the cup,
And into the hall, with gesture sad,
    For more would hold it up.

(87)

But now he cries, as the empty horn
 Into the hall he throws,
"A ship upon the sea is borne,
 Full heavily she goes ;
Now seemeth she to tarry,
 Now reacheth she the land ;
Two mighty giants carry
 The pale crew to the land."

O er ocean s wide dominions
 The Yarl now looketh he ;
"Those are Ellida's pinions—
 That, too, must Frithiof be :
By such a proud appearing
 Must Thorsten's son be known ;
In all the North, such bearing
 Belongs to him alone."

Forth from the board, in furious mood,
 Doth Viking Atle rise,
Black-bearded Berserk, craving blood,
 Rage flashing from his eyes :
"Now, now," he cries, "my hand shall show
 If Frithiof, as they say,
A spell o'er steel itself can throw,
 And ne'er for quarter pray."

With him sprung up twelve comrades there,
  Twelve comrades from the board ;
They wield the club, they cleave the air
  With fiercely-brandished sword.
They rush down to the level strand,
  Where rests the ship at length,
And Frithiof sitteth on the sand,
  Bespeaking might and strength.

" With ease my sword should fell thee now,"
  Doth boastful Atle cry,
" But that the choice I still allow
  To combat, or to fly.
Yet if thou'lt sue for peace from me
  (Though cruel name I bear),
Then, as a friend, I'll go with thee
  To noble Angantyr."

" My journey's toil hath left me weak,"
  Quoth Frithiof, fury-stirred ;
" Yet, ere a craven peace I seek,
  I'll prove thy mighty sword."
Flashes the steel with lightnings, flung
  From nervous, sunburnt hand ;
Each Rune on Angurvadel's tongue
  In burning flame doth stand.

The clashing weapons, showering, strike
  A hail of death-strokes round ;
The shattered shields of both alike
  Fall shivering to the ground.
Their comrades brave stand firm and fast,
  And none his place forsakes ;
Keen Angurvadel bites at last,
  The blade of Atle breaks.

" 'Gainst swordless man," bold Frithiof cried,
  " My sword I never use ;
But let us try another fight,
  If other fight thou choose."
Like floods, in autumn meeting,
  Each rusheth on his foe ;
Breastplate on breastplate beating,
  As they wrestle for the throw.

They wrestle, like an angry pair
  Of bears upon the snow ;
Like eagles, struggling high in air,
  Above the ocean's flow.
Have tottered from their ancient place
  Full many a massive rock,
And many an oak, of sturdy race,
  At far a slighter shock.

From heavy brows the sweat drops down,
  Their breath comes cold and hard ;
They scatter far each shrub and stone
  Around them on the sward.
To see the end, in fear delays
  Each troop upon the strand ;
Wide was that fight, in ancient days,
  Renown'd throughout the land.

But Frithiof felled his foe at last,
  And bore him to the earth,
And knelt upon his heaving breast,
  And spoke in tones of wrath :
" Oh ! had I but my broadsword true,
  Black-bearded Berserk, I
Should drive its point triumphant through
  Your entrails as you lie."

" Be that but little cause for care,"
  Was Atle's firm reply ;
" Go, fetch thy mighty weapon there,
  And no escape I'll try ;
We both must pass from earth away,
  Valhalla's joys to see ;
And if I wander there to-day,
  To-morrow may fetch thee."

Now, noble Frithiof, widely praised,
   The strife to finish thought,
Keen Angurvadel high he raised,
   But Atle trembled not.
This touched his mighty victor's soul,
   And laid his anger low ;
He checked the stroke, with glad control,
   And raised his fallen foe.

Then loud the agéd Halvar cried,
   His white staff raising forth :
" Through this your strife ye have supplied
   But little cause for mirth.
Long since the silver dishes high
   Send forth their steaming breath,
And fish and flesh grow cold, whilst I
   Am thirsting unto death."

Now reconciled, the warriors bold
   Pass through the open door,
And much did Frithiof there behold
   He ne'er had seen before.
No rough-hewn planks here cover
   The naked walls so wide ;
But leather, gilded over,
   With flowers and berries bright.

Not on the centre pavement glowed
   The fire, with merry glare,
But close by every wall there stood
   A stove of marble fair.
No smoke within the chamber stay'd ;
   The walls no dampness bore ;
Frames filled with glass the windows had,
   And a lock was on the door.

All filled with light, the branches fair
   Spread out their silver boughs ;
No more the crackling pine-torch glare
   Illumined the carouse.
Cooked whole, a stag, with larded breast,
   Adorned the table round ;
Its horns leaf-decked, its gilt hoof raised,
   As if about to bound.

There stood a damsel, lily-fair,
   To each rough comrade nigh ;
As beameth forth a glittering star
   Throughout a stormy sky.
Their tresses brown luxuriant flowed ;
   Bright shone their eyes of blue ;
Their little lips like roses glowed,
   Grown ripe in summer's dew.

High sate upon his silver throne
   The Yarl, in splendor bold ;
Bright as the sun his helmet shone,
   His breastplate blazed with gold ;
With stars embroider'd, bright did gleam
   His mantle, rich and fine ;
And every purple-glowing seam
   Did spotless ermine line.

Forth from the board three paces
   He goes to meet his guest ;
He takes his hand, and places
   Him at his side to rest :
" Since here full many a creaming horn
   With Thorsten emptied we,
His son, whose fame so far is borne,
   Shall not sit far from me."

The great Angantyr fills the cup
   With wine of Sicily ;
Like flashing flame it sparkles up
   All foaming, like the sea.
" Right welcome be thou to my hall
   In ancient friendship's name ;
The mighty Thorsten's skoal we all
   Shall drink with loud acclaim."

A hoary bard, from Morven's heights,
  Accords the tuneful lyre,
And loud, in glowing tones, recites
  A hero-song of fire ;
But in the old Norräna tongue,
  The speech of ancient days,
The hero Thorsten's fame was sung,
  And all the song did praise.

Then much to hear the Yarl did crave,
  Of his kindred in the North ;
And prudent Frithiof clearly gave
  The wisest answers forth.
And everything he truly tells,
  Gives each his proper fame,
Like Saga, goddess bright, who dwells
  In the shrine of holy Time.

And now doth Frithiof rehearse
  His voyage, lately done ;
How magic's power, and Helge's curse,
  By him had been o'erthrown.
The vassals shout in joyous strain,
  Loud laughs bold Angantyr,
And Frithiof greater glory gains
  As higher rose the cheer.

But when of Ingborg, dear and fair,
　The tale doth reach their ears,
So noble in her grief and care,
　So lovely in her tears,
Deep sighs escape from laboring breast,
　On fair cheeks blushes stand,
By every maiden fond is pressed
　Her faithful lover's hand.

And now, his mission to complete,
　Doth Frithiof bold prepare ;
Angantyr stirred not from his seat,
　But gave him hearing fair.
Then answered : " I no homage do ;
　I and my race are free ;
King Bele's skoal we drink, 'tis true,
　But he never governed me.

" His heirs, indeed, I never knew ;
　If tribute they demand,
Then let them sue as men should do,
　Insisting sword in hand.
Then on the shore my sword shall shine ;
　But Thorsten held I dear."
And with his hand he gives a sign
　To his daughter sitting near.

Up sprung the lovely Flower-charm
  Forth from her gilded chair ;
How slender was her little form,
  How round her bust so fair !
In dimple deep was throned the sprite
  Astril, in roguish glee,
As sits the butterfly so bright
  In the rose delightingly.

To the women's chambers hasting,
  She soon, with purse of green,
Returned, on which were rivers
  Through woods, embroidered seen.
And there displayed, the calm moonlight
  Seemed ocean to behold ;
The clasp was made of rubies bright ;
  The tassels were of gold.

The maiden laid the purse so fair
  In her great father's hands ;
Up to the brim he filled it there
  With gold from foreign lands :
" This gift of welcome take, O guest,
  To do as thou may'st will ;
But for the winter stay and rest
  With us in friendship still.

5

" Though valor never should be scorned,
  Yet now the storm rules wide ;
By now again to life return'ed,
  I'll wager Ham and Heyd.
Ellida may not always leap
  So luckily again ;
And whales are plenty in the deep,
  Though one she may have slain."

And so in merry mood they stay'd
  Till morning's sun did rise ;
The oft-drained golden goblets madé
  Them glad, but not unwise.
With skoal to Angantyr, at last,
  The horn they loudly drain ;
So, safely housed, till winter passed,
  Did Frithiof remain.

XII.

FRITHIOF'S RETURN.

SPRING breathes again in ether blue,
In green the earth is clad anew ;
Then Frithiof thanketh his host : again
He mounteth up on the heaving main ;
And gayly his sable swan doth make
On her glassy course a silvery wake.
For the western winds, with the voice of Spring,
Like nightingales in his bright sails sing ;
And the blue-veiled daughters of Œgir speed
His flight as they dance o'er the glittering mead.
Oh ! it is sweet when from distant strand
The sails swell back to that native land,
Where the smoke from one's own loved hearth ap-
    pears,
And thoughts awaken of childhood's years,—
Where play-grounds are mirrored in tranquil waves,
Where forefathers lie in their grassy graves ;
And the faithful maiden, longingly
Standing on lofty rocks, watcheth the sea.

Six days he sailed, and the seventh shows
A dark-brown stripe, which larger grows,
And 'gainst the edge of heaven doth stand,
With cliffs, with isles, and at last with land.
His home, from ocean risen, is seen,
Its forests wide arrayed in green ;
He hears the foaming surge's shocks
Break on the marble-breasted rocks ;
He greets the bay and the heights above,
And sails close under the holy grove,
Where the past summer, so many a night,
He had sat with his Ingborg in fond delight.
"Appeareth she not, and can she not guess
How near o'er the dark-blue waves I press ?
Or doth she, from Balder's temple gone,
Now dwelling at Helge's court alone,
Sorrow by harp, or by golden woof ? "

Lo ! his falcon now from the temple roof
Arising, as often before he hath done,
To Frithiof's shoulder hath suddenly flown,
Eagerly flapping with snowy wing,—
The bird from his shoulder can nobody bring.
With gilded claw he scratcheth in haste,—
He giveth no peace, he giveth no rest ;
To Frithiof's ear he bendeth his beak,
As if some message he sought to speak,

Perchance from Ingborg, the bride so dear,
But the tale he telleth can no man hear.

The last point now doth Ellida pass,
Bounding, as deer bound over the grass,
The well-known waters her keel doth plough,
Glad standeth Frithiof in the prow.
He rubbeth his eyes, and with trembling hand
He shadeth his brow, he scanneth the strand ;
But long though he rub them, and far though he see,
Framnäs no more discovereth he.
Nought but the naked chimney there
Standeth, like warriors' bones laid bare ;
Where his court-yard had been is desert land,
And ashes whirl round the lonely strand.
In fury down from his ship he hasteth ;
A glance on his ruined dwelling casteth,—
His father's dwelling—his childhood's home.

Now Bran, the wiry-haired, doth come,
His dog, who often, as true as bold,
For him the wild bears helped to hold ;
Full high he leapeth with many a spring,
In joy his master welcoming.
The milk-white steed, with the golden mane,
With stag-swift hoofs, and with lengthy rein,

Which Frithiof so often hath ridden around,
Speeds through the valley with eager bound,
And, neighing gladly, archeth his neck,
And bread from his master's hand doth seek.
But Frithiof, poorer than the pair,
Hath nought with the faithful brutes to share.
Houseless and sad, on his father's ground,
Now Frithiof standeth, gazing round ;
Until of Hilding he is 'ware,
His foster-sire, with silvery hair :
" At what I see I scarce can wonder ;
When the eagle flieth, the nest they plunder.
Is this the way that a king should guard ?—
Well holdeth Helge his royal word ;
For heavenly dread, and human hate,
And plundering flames, are his Eriksgate :
Yet this brings rather rage than care ;
But tell me, where is Ingborg ?—where ? "
" The tale I'll tell thee," the old man said ;
" Though I fear thou'lt find it but little glad :
Scarce wast thou gone when Ring drew near ;
Five shields to one his warriors were.
In Disar's vale by the brook they fought ;
With blood-red foam were its waters fraught.
King Halfdan, unchanging, laughed and played,
Yet wielded, like a man, his blade ;
Before the youth I held my shield,
And was proud of his well-fought maiden field.

Yet soon gave way our weakened host ;
King Helge fled, and then all was lost.
The Asen-born, as they swiftly fled,
Passing, in flames thy dwelling set.
No choice to the vanquished, Ring would leave :
Their sister they to him should give ;
Nought should appease him save her hand :
Refused, he'd seize both their crown and land.
Backwards and forwards the messengers hied ;
And now King Ring hath led home his bride."

"O woman ! woman !" Frithiof said,
"The earliest thought that Loke had
Was to frame a lie, and he sent it forth
In woman's form to man on earth.
With false blue eye, and with faithless tear,
Deceiving ever, yet ever dear ;
With rosy cheeks, and with bosom fair,
Thy faith like spring-ice, thy truth like air,
Thine heart but echoing with deceit,
And treachery set in thy lips so sweet.
O Ingborg, darling of my heart,
How dear thou hast been, and how dear thou art !
Far as I back my thoughts can guide,
I've known no joy but by thy side ;
In every act and in every thought,
Thou wast the highest prize I sought.

As trees from earth together grown,
If Thor with lightning smite the one,
The other fades ; if one grows green,
The other shares its leafy sheen :
So joy and care we've shared and known:
I never felt myself alone.
Now I am lonely ;—thou lofty Var,
Who, with thy golden tablets, far
Dost watch each mortal vow t' enrol,
Cease thy vain labor—burn thy scroll ;
But lies to chronicle they serve,
And better fate doth gold deserve.
Of Balder's Nanna truth is told,—
No truth can heart of mortal hold ;
Man's breast is filled with falsehood through,
Since Ingborg's voice could prove untrue ;
That voice, like wind caressing flowers,
Or strain from Brage's harp that showers,—
The joyous harp no more I'll hear,—
I'll think no more of my faithless fair.
Where storm-winds sport I'll make my pillow ;
Blood shalt thou quaff, thou ocean-billow !
Where'er a sword grave-seeds can sow,
O'er hill or dale, my joy shall grow ;
And meet I a crown'd king anywhere,
I'll laugh to see how his life I'll spare.
But should I find, where shields clash loud,
Some love-sick youth amongst the crowd,

Who joy in maiden's vows can take,
I'll hew him down for mercy's sake ;
And spare him the grief one day to be
Forsaken, disgraced, and betray'd like me."

" How fiercely boileth youthful blood !"
The aged Hilding said : " 'Twere good
That snows of eld should cool its heat.—
Much wrongest thou the noble maid :
My foster-daughter cease to chide,
But blame what none can turn aside,—
The rage of the Nornes, whose weapons smite
The sons of earth from the stormy height.
True ! Ingborg's sorrowing few men heard.
Like silent Vidar, she spake no word :
But she grieved and pined, as in southern shade
The love-lorn turtle-dove mourns its mate.
With me alone her grief she would share,
To me her measureless woe declare.
As with stricken breast the sea-mew diveth
To deepest ocean, and only striveth
To hide her wound from the sight of day,
And deep-laid, bleedeth her life away :
So in silence deep sank her sorrow down ;
To me only the grief that she bore is known.

"' For Bele's kingdom,' full oft she said,
' A sacrifice must I be made ;
5*

And garlands of snowdrops and evergreen
Shall deck the land's peace-offering.
Oh ! I could die, but 'twere fate too mild ;
By nought will Balder be reconciled
Save a living death of lingering pain,
With a beating heart, and a throbbing brain.
But to none of my sorrow, I charge thee, speak ;
My fate may be hard, yet no pity I seek ;
King Bele's daughter her doom will bear—
Yet greet from his Ingborg my Frithiof dear.'

" On the morn of the bridal (ah ! sad-fated day,
   From my runestaff, oh ! would I could score it
       away),
   To the temple passed the slow-pacing train
   Of white-cladden maidens, and sword-bearing men.
   By the sorrowing Skald the troop was led ;
   The bride sate pale on a coal-black steed,
   Pale as the spirit that sitteth upon
   The thunder-rack dark, when the storm rageth on.
   From the saddle I lifted the fair lily down ;
   To the temple-threshold I led her on ;
   By the altar standing, she uttered there
   Her vow to Lofn, and her voice was clear ;
   And she prayed to Balder fervently,
   And all wept tears, but no tear wept she.
   Of thy ring which she wore then was Helge 'ware,
   And he tore it with force from her arm so fair ;

And the image of Balder he decked with the gold.
My fury no longer could I withhold ;
My trusty sword from my side I drew forth,
And King Helge's life was then little worth.
But Ingeborg whispered me, ' Let things be ;
Such pang might a brother have spared to me ;
But much must be borne ere life's sorrows be past ;
Between us Allfader will judge at the last.' "

Quoth Frithiof : " Allfader judgeth, 'tis true,
But a share of judgment I'll utter too :
Is not to-night Balder's midsummer feast ?
I'll find in the temple that crown-wearing priest,—
That fire-raising king, who his sister could sell,
And my share of judgment shall please me well."

XIII.

BALDER'S BALE-FIRE.

M IDNIGHT sun on the mountains lay
  Blood-red to the sight ;
The air was filled with vapor gray
  Neither of day nor of night.

And Balder's pile, of the glowing sun
  A symbol true, blazed forth ;
But soon its splendor sinketh down
  When Höder rules the earth.

And round about the priests stood there,
  All busied with the brands,—
Pale-faced seers, with hoary hair,
  And flint-stone knives in horny hands.

Serving by the altar, crown'd,
  King Helge standeth near.
At midnight, hark ! through the grove around
  The clash of arms they hear.

" Björn, the portals guard, and so
    We'll captive take them all ;
In or out let no man go—
    Sooner cleave his skull."

Pale the king grew ; all too well
    He knew the voice for doubting :
In stalked Frithiof, furious, fell,
    Like autumn tempest shouting :

" Here's the tribute ; at thy desire
    I've fetched it o'er the sea ;
Take it ! and battle by Balder's fire
    For life and death with me.

" Shields on our backs, arms bare and free,
    Lest tame our strife be reckoned ;
Be the first stroke, as a king, to thee ;
    Remember, I have the second.

" Glance not, craven, at the door ;
    In cover I've trapped the fox ;
Think upon Framnäs—think, still more,
    On Ingborg's golden locks."

So valiant Frithiof spake with scorn,
    And carelessly did fling
The purse, from off his girdle torn,
    At the forehead of the king.

Blood from out his lips there oozed,
  Gloom took his sight away ;
By his altar, stunned and bruis'd,
  The god-descended lay.

" Thine own red gold canst thou not bear,
  Basest of Northmen, now ?
Then, shame for Angurvadel 'twere
  To fell such dross as thou.

" Avaunt, ye priests, with your altar knives—
  Pale moonshine princes curst,
Or little I'll reck to take your lives
  To quench my good sword's thirst.

" O ! Balder bright, forgive the harm ;
  Thine angry glances spare ;
Yon ring of gold upon thine arm
  Is nought but stolen ware.

" Never for thee, be it boldly said,
  'Twas forged by the great Valunder :
'Twas torn by a thief from a mourning maid :
  Away with his graceless plunder ! "

Boldly dragged he, but arm and ring
  Seemed to be grown the same,
Till, coming loose, the force doth fling
  The god into the flame.

Hark ! it crackles—the golden blaze
　　Reacheth the roof-tree fast ;
Björn, pale as death, at the portal stays,
　　Frithiof stands aghast.

" Let all men out—cast wide the door !
　　Thy watch no longer heed !
The temple flames !　Pour water—pour
　　The ocean-tide with speed !"

Down from the temple to the strand
　　They knit a chain of hands ;
The billows flow on from hand to hand,
　　And hiss upon the brands.

Like the god of rain doth Frithiof stand
　　High over beams and water,
And calmly gives each loud command
　　Midst flaming death's disorder.

In vain ! the flames gain the upper hand,
　　In smoke-wreaths rolled and swelled :
The gold drops into the glowing sand,
　　The plates of silver melt.

Now all is lost !　From the half-burnt hall
　　His flight a red cock wingeth,
And he percheth high on the gable tall,
　　And there wing-flapping clingeth.

The morning wind from the north hath hied,
　Far through the heavens blowing ;
Balder's grove is summer-dried,
　The flame is greedy and growing.

Fiercely it speedeth from tree to tree,
　A wide possession claiming.
Ha ! what a fierce, wild sight to see
　Great Balder's mighty flaming !

Down in each cleft root it crackleth still,
　High in each summit gloweth ;
'Gainst Muspel's ruddy sons, what skill
　Of man a barrier knoweth ?

A sea of flame fills Balder's ground,
　Strandless its billows stream ;
The sun mounts up, but fiord and sound
　Mirror forth nought but flame.

In ashes lies the temple's pride,
　The grove to ashes burneth,
And, wretched, Frithiof turns aside—
　Through morning hours he mourneth.

XIV.

FRITHIOF GOETH INTO BANISHMENT.

O N deck, by light
    Of summer night
Sat Frithiof grieving ;
Like ocean heaving,
His bosom sad
With awe and dread ;
Thick smoke still climbing
From the temple's flaming.

" To Valhall' fly
Through lofty sky,
Ye smoke-wreaths, seeking
Balder, bespeaking
His rage, just meed
To me decreed ;
Dread tidings giving
To echoing heaven

Of the temple bound
Razed to the ground ;
Of the image famed,
Which, falling, flamed,
And, charred away,
Like fire-wood lay.
Of the grove telling
(Religion's dwelling,
Where never sword
In strife was heard)
In ruins buried
By flames unwearied.
All that hath been,
All thou hast seen,
No jot forgetting.
Speed thou relating,
Envoy of cloud,
To the cloudy god.

" Mild Helge's glory
Shall live in story,
Not with his hand
Forth from the land
Me doth he banish ;
I yield, I vanish
O'er realms more wide
Of the azure tide.

Thou must not tarry,
Far must thou hurry,
Ellida forth
To the ends of earth ;
Fed in thy roaming
By ocean's foaming,
My dragon good,
A drop of blood
Can harm thee never ;
Speed thou on ever.
Where tempests roam
Thou art my home ;
The Asen-brother
Consumed the other.
Far must I wend
From fatherland ;
Be thou my North,
My foster-earth ;
Be thou my pride,
Thou dark-robed bride ;
False was my other
Bride to her lover.

" Free-flowing sea !
No trouble to thee
Is monarch's grieving,
Or king's deceiving.

He only can be
King over thee
Who never feareth,
Though lofty reareth
Thy foaming breast,
Its billows tost.
Thine azure furrows
Are tilled by heroes ;
Through them, like plough,
The keel doth go.
'Neath oak's wide shadow
Blood dews the meadow.
Sown is death's seed
From bright steel shed.
Who ocean reapeth,
Thence glory keepeth,—
Gold cometh too ;
To me be true,
Thou stormy billow ;
And I will follow.

" My father's grave
Stands still and safe ;
Calm waters mirror
His grass-green pillow.
Blue shall mine be
In the foaming sea ;

Sturdily floating,
Midst tempests shouting,
Till I sink to sleep
In the boundless deep.
My life art thou, ocean—
My home, my possession ;
And shalt be my grave,
Free-flowing wave."

So spake he madly,
As piloting sadly
His vessel, he bore
Forth from the shore ;
And coasted slowly
The headlands holy,
Which still stand forth,
Guarding the North.
But vengeance waketh :
With ten ships seeketh
King Helge wight
To check his flight.
Then shouted they all,
" Now Helge will fall :
He offereth strife,
Nor careth for life
Here 'neath the moon.
This Valhall's son

Doth long to rise
To native skies ;
And, kin to the gods,
Seeketh Odin's abode."

Scarce was this said,
When Helge's fleet,
By unseen power,
Sank lower and lower ;
Still sinking on,
Till settled down
Midst Rana's dead.
Swimming, in dread,
Doth Helge reach
Alone the beach.

Björn, loud laughed he,
And quoth merrily :
" Thou of Odin's blood,
My craft was good ;
When none was nigh,
Thy ships bored I
Last night with speed,—
A worthy deed !
May Rana keep
Them in the deep,

As is her wont ;
I but lament
That from the wave
Thou shouldst be safe."

On rocky shore,
His peril o'er,
King Helge stood
In wrathful mood ;
His bow, ere long,
Of steel, he strung,
And scarcely knew
How far he drew,
Till with a twang
In twain it sprang.

But Frithiof stayed
His lance, and said :
"Thy death-bird here
Enchained I bear ;
O coward king,
If I freed its wing,
Low shouldst thou lie
For thy villainy.
Yet ease thy fears ;
My lance ne'er cares

For cowards' blood ;
She's far too good
For such base uses ;
And rather chooses
Her sign to grave
On tombs of the brave,
Than on pillars of shame,
Where is branded thy name.—
Thy fame on sea
Is lost to thee ;
And e'en on earth
'Tis little worth.
Rust snapped thy bow,
Not strength, I trow ;
At nobler game
Than thee I aim,—
'Twere shame to me
To slaughter thee."

Then bent he o'er
The sturdy oak,
Once pine-tree tall
In Gudbrand's vale.
He grasped its fellow,
And o'er the billow
He rode with speed ;
Like bending reed,

Or broadsword's tongue,
The stout oars sprung.

Up rose the sun,
On the cliffs he shone ;
And the breeze, speeding
From shore, seemed bidding
Each wave to dance
In morning's glance.
O'er the billow's crest
Ellida pressed
Merrily and glad ;
But Frithiof said :

" Crest of creation,
    Thou noble North,
I have no place on
    Thy well-loved earth ;
From thee forever
    My sail must swell ;
Thou nurse of valor,
    Farewell ! farewell !

" Farewell, thou brightest
    Valhalla-throne ;
Thou gloom that lightest,
    Midsummer sun !

6

Thou sky, unclouded,
Where heroes dwell,
Where bright stars wander,
Farewell ! farewell !

" Ye mighty cliffs,
Famed evermore,
Rune-written temples
Of terrible Thor :
Each azure sea
That I've known so well,
Each isle and bay,
Farewell ! farewell !

" Farewell, ye graves
By the ocean's foam,
Where the linden-tree waves
Down its snowy bloom,
(But Saga judgeth,
And judgeth well
What earth concealeth,)
Farewell ! farewell !

" Farewell, each grove,
And each grassy nook,
Where I loved to lie
By the rippling brook.

Friends of my youth,
I loved you well ;
But we part forever—
Farewell ! farewell !

" With fondness spurned,
With honor stained,
With dwelling burned,
And banishment :
From land I part
O'er ocean's swell—
Ah ! joy of heart,
Farewell ! farewell ! "

XV

VIKINGABALK.

NOW wide swept he round on the wilderness deep;
    he sped far, like the prey-seeking hawk,
For his comrades on board he wrote counsel and law;
    wilt thou hear now his Vikingabalk?

" Make no tent upon deck, sleep not under a roof,
    within doors a foe may surprise :
On his shield Viking sleepeth, his sword in his
    hand, and maketh his tent of the skies.

" Short shaft hath the hammer of conquering Thor;
    a sword but an ell long hath Frey;
'Tis enough, for thy sword can be never too short,
    hast thou heart to thy foe to come nigh.

" When the storms rage with might, hoist the sail to
    its height, then are merry the storm-ridden
    waves ;

(124)

Speed along! speed along! and sink sooner than
 strike, for they who would strike are but
 slaves!

"Shelter woman on land; keep her far from your
 bark—she'd deceive, ay, though Freya she
 were:
For her dimple so deep is a pitfall untrue, and a
 net is her wide-waving hair.

"Wine is Valfader's drink, and carouse is allowed, if
 thou drainest uninjured the can;
If thou fallest on land, thou may'st rise; but fall
 here, and thou sinkest to sleep-giving Ran.

"When a merchant sails by, spare his ship; by the
 weak let a tribute for safety be told;
Thou art king on thy waves, he a slave to his gain,
 and thy steel is as good as his gold.

"By the die and the lot all your prizes divide; how
 they fall, to complain never care;
Your sea-king himself casteth never a lot, keepeth
 only his fame as his share.

"Comes a Vikinga-ship, and we board it and fight,
 when the strife waxeth hot 'neath each shield,

If thou yield but a pace, thou art parted from us ;
 'tis our law, and so do as thou wilt.

" Hast thou conquered ? Give grace—he's no longer
  a foe, who defenceless for mercy doth pray ;
Pale Prayer is Valhalla's child ; yield to its voice ;
  he is worthless who then sayeth Nay.

" Scars are gain to a Viking ; a man they adorn, if
  on brow or on bosom they stand ;
Let them bleed on unbound until evening be come ;
  if not, thou must part from our band."

So wrote he his law, and his fame day by day to
  far-lying borders was brought ;
His like never sped o'er the blue heaving sea, and
  his comrades full lustily fought.

But himself by the tiller sat, gloomy of mien, and
  gazed into ocean, and thought :
" Deep art thou ; in thy depths, perhaps, peace may
  be found, but above I discover it not.

" If the White One still rage, let him draw forth his
  blade ; I'll fall gladly, if so 'tis designed ;
But he sitteth in heaven, and sendeth down thoughts
  that darken forever my mind."

Still, when battle drew near, like an eagle refreshed
    rose his spirit in valorous flight,
And clear grew his brow, and high raised he his
    voice, and stood forth like the Thunderer
    bright.

So from conquest to conquest he sped, and from
    care, in the ocean he sought for release,
And islands and cliffs passed he southward, and
    so came he into the waters of Greece.

As his glance on the groves rising up from the sea,
    and the temples, now desolate, fell,
What he felt Freya knew, and the bard, too, must
    know ; and ye, lovers, ye know it full well.

" Here should we have dwelt ; here the isle, here the
    grove, here the temple my sire shadowed
    forth ;
It was hither I prayed my beloved to come ; but
    the cruel one stayed in the North.

" Doth contentment not dwell in yon valley of bliss,
    and peace round those pillars so strong ?
Like the whispers of love sounds the murmuring
    brook, like a bride-hymn the nightingale's
    song.

"Where is Ingeborg now? Hath she e'er thought
    of me, with her agéd spouse withered and
    gray?
I ne'er can forget; but to see her once more, my
    whole life I'd give gladly away.

"Three years have sped by since my home I beheld,
    great Saga's majestical hall;
Stand forth still 'gainst the heaven her bright cliffs
    on high? groweth green still my ancestors'
    vale?

"On the mound, where my father is laid, did I plant
    a linden-tree—bloometh it now?
Who hath tended it since? Give it nurture, O
    Earth, and thy dew on it, Sky, sprinkle
    thou.

"Yet why lie I longer on billows afar, for slaughter
    and plundering prize?
I have honor enough, and the red-flaming gold,
    the worthless, my soul doth despise.

"The flag on my mast streameth back to the North;
    to the North, to my fatherland dear;
I'll follow the course of the heavenly winds; back
    again to my Northland I'll steer."

XVI.

FRITHIOF AND BJÖRN.

FRITHIOF.

BJÖRN, I am weary of wave and of sea ;
  Boisterous comrades the billows have proved ;
Far in the North the proud headlands beloved
Back, with resistless might, beckon to me.
They are happy from home who have never departed,
Ne'er banished afar from their ancestors' graves !
Too long, alas ! all too long broken-hearted,
I've wandered around on the wide-heaving waves.

BJÖRN.

Good is the ocean, in vain dost thou chide ;
Freedom and gladness thrive best on the seas ;
Little they reck of effeminate ease
Loving afar on the billows to ride.
When I grow old, upon land I will house,
And cling in my turn to it, close as the grass ;
But now in hot battle and joyous carouse,
On ocean, my swift years untroubled shall pass.

6*

FRITHIOF.

Yet now by the ice we are driven to land,
Clasping our keel lie the chilly waves dead ;
Nor care I to wait till long winter be sped,
Imprisoned by rocks on the desolate strand.
Once more in the Northland my Yule-tide I'll hold,
And guest to King Ring and my lost bride will be ;
Gaze fondly again on those bright locks of gold,
And hear once again that voice dearest to me.

BJÖRN.

Good is thy purpose.—By Ring shall be seen
How vengeance of Viking like lightning can gleam :
At midnight the court of the monarch shall flame :
We'll slaughter the Graybeard, we'll bear off the
　　　　Queen.
Or wilt thou treat him in Vikinga-wise,
Hold'st thou him worthy of Holm-gang with thee ?
Then challenge him forth to contend on the ice ;
Whatever thou willest, I ready shall be.

FRITHIOF.

Speak not of slaughter, nor think upon war ;
In peace to the court of the monarch I'll wend.
Faultless is he, nor did Ingborg offend,
But the vengeance of angry gods I have to bear.
Now leave of my dear one my heart longs to take,
Since slight hope for me upon earth can remain ;

A farewell eternal ! when green buds awake
At the breathing of spring, thou shalt see me again.

BJÖRN.

Ah ! Frithiof, thy folly seems strange to my mind :
What ! sorrow and sigh for a false woman's love !
In sooth, upon earth there are women enough !
For the one thou hast lost thou a thousand may'st find.
If thou wilt, e'en a lading of that kind of ware
Shall swiftly from Southland so glowing be brought,
As ruddy as rosebuds, like lambs tame and fair ;
We'll divide them as brothers, or share them by lot.

FRITHIOF.

Björn, glad and honest as Frey is thy thought :
Thou art prudent in counsel, and fearless in war ;
Well hast thou learnt to know Odin and Thor,
But Freya, the heavenly, knowest thou not.
Shun to think scorn of the holy Queen's power ;
Beware, lest the rage of the goddess thou wake ;
To gods and to men, soon or late, comes the hour
When her mouldering spark into fierce flame must
    break.

BJÖRN.

Yet go not alone.   They may take thee in thrall.

FRITHIOF.

Alone go I not ; my sword followeth me.

BJÖRN.

Remember how Hagbart was hung on a tree.

FRITHIOF.

He, who lets any take him, deserveth to fall.

BJÖRN.

Oh ! brother, fall'st thou, I'll avenge thee full well :
Over Frithiof's bones the blood-eagle I'il tear.

FRITHIOF.

It needeth not, Björn.   For my foeman shall ne'er
Hear a cock crow again when I perish.   Farewell !

XVII

FRITHIOF COMETH TO KING RING.

KING RING high-throned at banquet sat, mead-
        quaffing at Yule-tide ;
The fair and gentle-visaged queen sat silent by his
        side ;
Like Spring by Autumn seated, they seemed together
        there :
In her was seen the Spring-time green, in him the
        Autumn drear.

And lo ! into the hall there came an unknown gray-
        beard in,
From head to foot enveloped in a wild bear's shaggy
        skin ;
With weak and weary gait upon his heavy staff he
        leant,
Still all the rest surpassing in stature as he went.

(133)

He sat him on the lowly bench that stood beside
    the door,
That is the poor man's place to-day, as 'twas in
    days of yore ;
To mock with sneer and scornful laugh the under-
    lings began,
And pointed with the finger at the rude, uncouth,
    old man.

Forth flashed the ready fury from the stranger's
    eyes ; in haste,
With a single hand he snatcheth up a courtier by
    the waist,
And thoughtfully upon his head he turned the
    frightened youth,
Then all the others held their peace—as we'd have
    done, in sooth.

'What means, below, this uproar—who dares our
    peace to break ?
Come up to me, thou graybeard, and answer when
    I speak :
What is thy name ?—what wilt thou ?—and where
    thy fatherland ? "
So spake the angry monarch ; calm did the old man
    stand.

" Full much thou askest me, O king, yet answer will
    I give :
Trouble thyself not for my name, its master still
    doth live ;
The land of sorrow is my home ; my birthright,
    misery ;
Last night I lodged with hungry wolves ; thence
    come, to-day, to thee.

" In days gone by full glad I rode on ocean-dragon
    free,
And mighty were the wings she had, and merrily
    sped she ;
But now she lieth frozen up and lame upon the
    sand,
While I myself, grown old and weak, burn salt
    upon the strand.

" I came to see thy wisdom, by fame so widely
    borne ;
Those yonder mocked me scornfully, and I'm too
    old for scorn ;
I seized upon a grinning fool, and turned him up-
    side down,
Yet all unharmed he rose again ; so, king, no
    longer frown."

"Not ill-beseeming," quoth the king, "thy bold
    words are to thee,
And age should all men honor; come, sit thee
    down by me;
Let's see thee frank and freely; let thy thick cover-
    ing fall:
Disguise disturbs enjoyment, and I wish joy to
    all."

Then straightway from his head the guest let fall
    the rugged hide,
And in the old man's place they all a noble youth
    espied;
Down from his lofty forehead, o'er his broad shoul-
    ders' might,
Fell down, like waves of molten gold, his locks in
    splendor bright.

In azure velvet mantle stood he, gorgeously ar-
    rayed,
With silver belt, a hand in width, and beasts there-
    on displayed,
Fiercely their prey pursuing around the hero's
    waist,
By some laborious master in high-wrought beauty
    chased.

Around his mighty arm he wore a golden bracelet
    wide,
Like a flash of bridled lightning hung his war-sword
    at his side ;
A royal, fearless glance around the hall and guests
    he bore,
And stood, like Balder beauteous, brave and proud
    as mighty Thor.

Swift to the gentle queen's pale cheeks the crimson
    color sped ;
So, 'neath the glow of northern lights, wide plains
    of snow blush red ;
And, as twin water-lilies, by sudden storm op-
    pressed,
Flutter above the billows, so heaved her gentle
    breast.

The horn was blown for silence, come was the
    votive hour ;
To Frey's high feast devoted they carry in the
    boar ;
Its shoulders decked with flowers, its mouth an
    apple held,
And, with knees beneath it bended, the silver dish
    it filled.

Then slowly agéd Ring raised up his venerable
    head,
He touched the forehead of the boar, and vowing,
    thus he said :
" Great Frithiof I will vanquish, whom none can
    stand before,
So help me, Frey and Odin, and so help me, mighty
    Thor ! "

With haughty mien the stranger rose up quickly
    from his seat,
His countenance all glowing with heroic anger's
    heat ;
He struck his sword upon the board, the hall re-
    echoing rang,
And up from every oaken seat each startled com-
    rade sprang.

" Now hear thou, too, O king ! " he cried, " my vow,
    thus uttered loud,
That Frithiof is akin to me, a worthy friend and
    good ;
And Frithiof I will shelter against all the world
    arrayed,
So help me first my favoring Norne, and then my
    trusty blade ! "

" Thou speakest boldly," smiled the king, " nor only
    once to-day ;
But frank and free each word shall be where I, as
    king, bear sway.
Fill, consort mine, the horn with wine, and fill it
    of the best ;
This stranger, let us hope, will bide the winter as
    our guest."

Then took the queen the horn that on the board
    before her stood,
(Which Ure's forehead once adorned, a treasure
    rich and good,)
On feet of shining silver, with many a gold ring
    bound,
Rune-written, and with deeds of ancient days be-
    decked around.

And as she offered him the horn, all trembling, with
    averted head,
The goblet shook, some drops ran o'er, and dyed
    her fingers rosy red ;
And as upon the lily leaves the sunset glories seem
    to stand,
So glowed the drops of purple wine upon the fair
    one's snowy hand.

With joy from her the stranger took the horn, and
    raised it high ;
Two men (such men as live to-day) could scarce
    have drunk it dry ;
But the mighty guest, deep-quaffing in honor of the
    queen,
Drained the full goblet at a draught,—no drop re-
    mained within.

Then the bard who sat at the board of royal Ring
    his harp drew forth,
And a beautiful sorrowful song did sing of true love
    in the North,—
Of Hagbart and fair Signe : and at the mournful
    tale,
The hard heart melted in each breast beclad in
    shining mail.

He sang of the halls of Valhalla, the Einherier's
    praise sang he,
Of valiant forebears' mighty deeds on continent
    and sea ;
Then every hand its sword-hilt clutched, and bright
    flashed every eye,
And round and round the oft-filled horn sped ever
    busily.

Deep drank they, high carousing, at the palace of
    the king,
And reveller good each proved himself at Yule-tide
    banqueting ;
Then staggered forth to slumber, unmoved by woe
    or care,
But Ring, the agéd monarch, stayed with Ingeborg
    the fair.

XVIII.

THE RIDE OVER THE ICE.

KING RING to a banquet with Ingeborg hies ;
The ice on the bay like a mirror lies.

" Sledge not over the ice," the stranger cried ;
" 'Twill break, and too deep is the frozen tide."

Quoth Ring : " Not so easily kings are drowned ;
Whoever's afraid, by the shore may go round."

How frowneth the stranger in angry heat !
He bindeth his steel shoes in haste to his feet.

How starteth the stallion forth with might,
Fierily snorting in fierce delight !

" Stride out," Ring crieth, " my charger good !
Let's see that thou art of Sleipner's blood."

They speed as storms over ocean speed :
The queen's prayers little King Ring doth heed.

Their steel-shod comrade standeth not still,
He flieth past them as swift as he will.

Many a Rune on the ice cutteth he ;
Fair Ingborg's name discovereth she.

So on their glittering course they go,
But Ran, the traitress, lurketh below.

A hole in her silver roof she hath reft,
Down sinketh the sleigh in the yawning cleft.

How pale groweth Ingeborg's cheek with fear !
The guest, like a whirlwind, cometh near :

His skate he hath fixed on the icy field ;
The steed by the mane he hath seized and held ;

With a single tug he setteth amain
Both steed and sleigh on the ice again.

" Praise to that stroke," quoth Ring, " is due ;
Not Frithiof, the mighty, could better do."

Now turn they back to the court again ;
Till spring the stranger doth there remain.

XIX

FRITHIOF'S TEMPTATION.

SPRING-TIME cometh; wild birds twitter, woods
grow leafy, sunshine beams,
Dancing, singing, down to ocean speed the liberated
streams;
Out from its bud the glowing rose peeps forth like
blush on Freya's cheek;
And joy of life, and mirth, and hope, within the
breast of man awake.

The agéd monarch wills the chase, and with him hies
the gentle queen;
And swarming round in proud array is all the court
assembled seen:
Bows are twanging, quivers rattle, eager horse-hoofs
paw the clay;
And, with hooded eyes, the falcons scream impatient
for their prey.

Lo ! the chase's empress cometh ! Hapless Frithiof,
    glance away !
Like a star on spring cloud sitteth she upon her
    courser gray,
Half like Freya, half like Rota, lovelier than the
    heavenly pair ;
From her slender hat of purple azure plumes float
    high in air.

Gaze not on her eyes so beauteous, on her golden
    locks so bright,
Gaze not on her form so slender, on her bosom full
    and white ;
Shun to watch the rose and lily on her soft cheek
    varying ;
Hark not to the voice belovéd, breathing like the
    sighs of spring.

Now the hunter's troop is ready. Hallo ! over hill
    and dale
Horns reëcho ; eager falcons climb aloft to Odin's
    hall :
All the forest beasts affrighted seek their distant lairs
    in fear ;
But with lance outstretched before her, their Valkyria
    follows near.

7

Ring the agéd cannot follow as the chase speeds
    swiftly on,
Sorrowful and silent by him rideth Frithiof
    alone,
Gloomy, mournful recollections all his soul with
    anguish tear,
And, wherever he can turn him, hears he echoes
    of despair.

" Wherefore fled I from the ocean, to mine own de-
    struction blind ?
Sorrow thrives not on the billow, far 'tis blown by
    heaven's wind.
If Viking broodeth, danger comes, and bids him to
    the sprightly dance,
And his gloomy bodings vanish, blinded by his
    weapon's glance.

" Far otherwise 'tis here : for grief unspeakable has
    thrown
Her dark wings round my forehead; like a dreamer
    pass I on :
Never can I Balder's grove, or Ingborg's loving
    oath forget,
Sworn to me.—SHE never broke it ; gods, in fury,
    cancelled it.

" They, the race of man detesting, jealous view a
    fondness blest ;
My rose-bud sweet they snatched away, and planted
    it in Winter's breast :
By its bloom can Winter profit?   Little knoweth he
    its price ;
While his frosty breathing covers bud, and leaf, and
    stem with ice."

While thus he sorrowed, they their way into a
    lonely dell had made,—
Dark and hill-surrounded, overspread with birch
    and alder shade.
Ring, dismounting, quoth : " How cool and pleas-
    ant doth the grove appear !
Weary am I ; let us rest, and for an hour I'll slum-
    ber here."

" Here thou may'st not sleep, O king, for such a
    slumber bringeth pain ;
Up ! The ground is hard and cold—full soon I'll
    lead thee home again."
" Like other gods," the old man said, " sleep cometh
    when we hope it least,
And surely to his host my guest will scarce be-
    grudge a little rest ? "

Then Frithiof took his mantle off, and spread it out
    beneath the trees,
And trustfully the old king laid his head upon the
    young man's knees,
Slept soundly, as upon his shield a warrior after
    war's alarms,
And softly as an infant sleeps within its mother's
    loving arms.

As he slumbers, hark ! there sings a coal-black bird
    from off a bough :
" Haste thee, Frithiof, slay the Graybeard—end thy
    sorrows at a blow !
Take the queen—she's thine, since once to thee
    betrothal's kiss she gave :
Here no mortal eye beholds thee ; deep and silent
    is the grave."

Frithiof listens,—hark ! now sings a snow-white
    bird from off a bough :
" Though no mortal eye behold thee, Odin's eye can
    see thee now :
Coward ! wouldst thou murder sleep ? Shall help-
    less age by thee be slain ?
Such deed, whate'er to thee it bring, can never
    peace or honor gain."

So the birds sang, both in turn, but Frithiof took
    his battle-blade,
Shuddering he flung it from him, far into the
    gloomy shade ;
The black bird back to Nastrand flies ; but, borne
    along on shining wings,
With song as sweet as tuneful harp, the white one
    up to sunshine springs.

Straight the old king, waking, quoth : " Much rest
    did my short sleep afford ;
'Tis sweet to slumber in the shade, protected by a
    brave man's sword :
But where, O stranger, is thy blade—the lightning's
    brother, whither sped ?
And who hath separated you, so little wont to sepa-
    rate ?"

" It matters little," Frithiof said, "for swords are
    plenty in the North ;
Sharp-tonguéd is the blade, O king ; no word of
    peace it speaketh forth :
Within the steel doth evil dwell, a spirit dark from
    Niffelhem ;
Against him sleep no safety hath ; gray hairs are
    but a snare to him."

" Dissembled was my slumber, youth, to prove thee,"
    agéd Ring replied ;
" The wise should never trust himself to man or
    sword of man untried.
Thou art Frithiof; when my hall thou entered'st I
    knew thee well :
Old Ring hath long been ᵓ ware of what his guest
    sought to conceal.

" Wherefore, thus disguised and nameless, 'neath my
    roof-tree didst thou glide ?
Wherefore ? Was it from the old man's arms to
    steal away his bride ?
Honor, Frithiof, never sitteth nameless at the ban-
    quet gay ;
Frank and open is its visage, and its shield is
    bright as day.

" The dread alike of gods and men, to me a Frithiof
    far was famed ;
Shields he cleft ; by him insulted, sacred shrines in
    ruin flamed ;
Soon with fierce array he'll come, I ever thought, to
    vex my land,
And he came,—in beggar's raiment, and a staff was
    in his hand.

" Yet, wherefore turn away thy gaze ?   I, too, have
      felt youth's angry strife ;
It is the time of Berserk-rage in each man's ever-
      struggling life :
In clash of arms its course must pass, until ap-
      peased its fierce mood be :
Thy fault in pity I forget, since I have proved and
      pardoned thee.

" Thou seest I am agéd grown, and to the grave must
      soon decline ;
Then take to thee my realm, and take the queen,
      for she is thine.
Meanwhile, remain, my son, and dwell within my
      palace as before ;
Guard me, thou swordless warrior ; our ancient
      strife is o'er."

" Never," gloomy Frithiof answered, " came I as a
      thief to thee ;
And had I willed to take thy queen, could any man
      have hindered me ?
I only longed my bride to see but once—alas ! but
      once again,
And, woe is me ! the half-quenched flame rekindled
      I to fiercer pain.

" Too long within thy halls I've stayed, and now no
     further linger I ;
Full heavily upon my head the rage of angry gods
     doth lie ;
For Balder, with the radiant locks, who all mar-
     kind besides doth see
With love, detesteth me alone, and me alone reject-
     eth he.

" 'Tis true, I caused his shrine to flame, and Varg-i-
     Veum call they me ;
To hear my name the children scream, and glad-
     ness from the feast doth flee ;
Its offspring lost, my Fatherland with indignation
     forth doth cast,
And I am peaceless in my home, and peaceless in
     my mourning breast.

" No more, no more for peace in vain I'll seek upon
     the grassy earth ;
Beneath my footsteps burns the soil, no shade to
     me the trees give forth ;
My Ingeborg is lost to me, alas ! by agéd Ring
     she's owned ;
Life's sun for me is set, and wide is sorrow's dark-
     ness spread around.

" And, therefore, to my waves again.   Away, away,
  my dragon good,
Thy sable breast plunge merrily once more into the
  briny flood ;
Spread to the clouds thy pinions bright, the hissing
  ocean proudly tear,
And fly as far as stars can lead, as swift as conquered waves can bear.

" Let me hear the storm tremendous, let me hear
  fierce thunder's voice ;
When tumultuous din surrounds me, calmly can
  my breast rejoice.
In clang of shields and hail of arrows be my furious
  sea-fights passed,
Till glad I fall, and rise, forgiven, to the gods ap-
  peased at last."

XX.

THE DEATH OF KING RING.

WITH golden mane gleaming,
Skinfaxe more nobly
Draweth the sun from the waves than before ;
Morning's bright beaming
Illumineth doubly
The hall of the monarch ; then opens the door.

Gloomy and grieving
Frithiof seeketh
The king ; pale he sitteth ; fair Ingeborg's breast
Like ocean is heaving ;
The stranger he speaketh
Words of departure, in trembling expressed :

" The blue billows chafe
My swift-wingéd steed,
My sea-courser longeth to bound from the strand ;
He doth pine for the wave,
So forth I must speed,
Forth from dear friends, and away from the land.

(154)

" This ring take—thine own again,
    Ingborg ; there liveth
Holy remembrance within it for thee ;
    Give it to none again ;
    Frithiof forgiveth,
But now never more on earth seest thou me.

" Smoke ne'er shall I see
    Ever rising again
Forth from the North.   Man is only a slave
    To what Nornas decree ;
    The wave-tossing main
Henceforth is my fatherland, shall be my grave.

" Thy bride to the strand,
    O Ring, shun to take,
Above all, when the starlight illumines the sky ;
    For, perchance, on the sand,
    By ocean cast back,
The course of the wandering Viking may lie."

Then quoth the king :
    " 'Tis bitter to hear
A man thus lament, like a sorrowing maid ;
    Full long doth Fate sing
    Her dirge in my ear ;
What matters it ?   All that is mortal must fade.

" Norna's decreeing,
        However it fall,
Strive we, or grieve we, we cannot withstand.
        To thee leave I my queen,
        And my power, and all,
So thou guard for my young heir his ancestors' land.

    " To many friends spake I
        Full oft in the hall,
And golden peace ever loved truly and well ;
        Yet often, too, brake I
        Shields in the vale,
Shields on the wave, and I never grew pale.

    " Now will I carve amain
        Geirsodd, and, bleeding,
No straw-death, ill-seeming a king, I'll receive ;
        Nor is the parting pain
        Worth monarch's heeding ;
It scarce can be harder to die than to live."

    So carveth he sprightly
        Letters for Odin,
Into bosom and arm the deep death-runes are press'd ;
        Shining forth brightly,
        Thick blood-drops flowed on,
Trickling through silver hairs over his breast.

" Reach forth the horn ;
      Loud skoal shall arise
Skoal to thy glory, thou beautiful North !
      Plentiful corn,
         And counsellors wise,
And labor in peace for thee sought I on earth.

" Vainly and wildly
      In conquest I sought her,
Sought I for peace, who still further did flee ;
      Now stands she mildly,
         The grave's gentle daughter,
At the feet of the gods she is waiting for me.

" Hail, ye deities bright !
      Ye Valhalla sons !
Earth fadeth away ; to the heavenly feast
      Glad trumpets invite
         Me, and blessedness crowns,
As fair, as with gold helm, your hastening guest."

So spake he, pressing
      The hand of his spouse,
Greeting his sorrowing friend and his son ;
      And then, his eyes closing,
         Ring's spirit arose,
And sped on a sigh up to Allfather's throne.

XXI.

RING'S DRAPA.

IN the grave sitteth
   Ring, greatest of monarchs ;
Beside him his battle-sword,
Shield on his arm ;
His charger, the noble,
Neighing beneath him,
With gilded hoof paweth
The wall of his grave.

Richly now rideth
Ring over Bifrost ;
Arched is the bridge
Which to meet him descends ;
Wide spring the portals
Of noble Valhalla,
Gods grasping, rejoicing,
The chief by the hand.
(158)

Thor is not present,
Far off he warreth ;
Valfader beckons,
The beaker is brought ;
The crown of the monarch
With corn-ears Frey decketh ;
And flowers among them
Doth Frigga entwine.

Bragé, the aged,
Sweepeth the harp-strings,
Sweeter than ever
The tones of his song.
Vanadis, listening,
O'er the board leaneth ;
Glowing, her snowy
Bosom doth heave.

" High sing the clashing
Of sword upon helmet,
Murmuring billows,
Heaving in blood :
And might, the good gift
Of the happy immortals,
Which, keenly as Berserk,
Biteth the shield.

" Therefore, by us was
 Ring well-beloved :
 His shield ever guarding
 Regions of peace.
 Whence the loveliest image
 Of might unoffending,
 Before us, like incense,
 Forever arose.

" Words of deep wisdom
 Valfader speaketh,
 Sitting by Saga,
 Söquabäck's maid.
 So the words sounded
 Of Ring ever clearly,
 As Mimer's bright billows,—
 Deep, too, as they.

" Peaceful Forsete,
 Feud-reconciling,
 Ruleth by Urda's
 Aye-heaving wave.
 So on the Ting-stone
 Sat the wise monarch,
 Appeasing the rage of
 Avengers of blood.

" Ne'er was he niggardly :
Round him he scattered
(From Dragon's bed gathered)
The daylight of dwarfs.
Gifts sped forth gladly
From hand ever open ;
And comfort for grief
From his lips ever fell.

" Welcome, thou wise one,
Heir of Valhalla !
Long in the Northland
Liveth thy fame.
Bragé, with greeting,
Draineth the mead-horn
To thee, the Norne's herald
Of peace from the North !"

XXII.

THE KING'S ELECTION.

TO the Ting ! the Ting ! Budkafle goes
    From home to home :
King Ring is dead. A king to choose
    The Northmen come.

From idle wall is ta'en the brand
    Of purple steel :
Each warrior, with practised hand,
    Its edge doth feel.

The little sons behold with joy
    Its glitter bright :
Two raise it up, for either boy
    Too heavy weight.

The daughter scrubs the helmet clean,
    Bright must it glare ;

6*   (162)

Then blushes red, for she has seen
    Her image there.

He taketh, last of all, his shield,—
    A sun in blood.
Hail to thee, freeborn warrior, mailed,
    Thou yeoman good !

From thy free breast alone can grow
    A nation's pride ;
In war, thy country's rampart thou ;
    In peace, its guide.

Assembled round, with warlike cry,
    In proof arrayed,
Their weapons clash ; the heaven high
    Their tent is made.

And Frithiof stands upon the judging-stone,
    And with him there
A little child, the late king's only son,
    With golden hair.

There passed a murmur through the people far :
    " Too young is he
To judge our wrongs, and of our hosts in war
    The chief to be."

Up on his shield set Frithiof bold
  The child, and cried :
" Here, Northmen, stands your king ! Behold
  The Northland's pride !

" See how, with Odin's likeness filled,
  And fair as he ;
He standeth bold, on slippery shield,
  As fish in sea.

" With sword and steel will I defend
  His realm's renown,
And round the child's young brow will bend
  The father's crown.

" Forsete, son of Balder bright,
  Record my vow,
And lay me, ere its bond I slight,
  In darkness low."

Shield-thronéd sat, with fearless eye,
  Ring's royal son,
As eagles' young, from eyrie high,
  Gaze on the sun.

But Time's course, to the child's young blood,
  Seemed far too slow ;

With royal bound, in courage proud,
    He sprung below.

Loud rose the shout through all the Ting:
    "We Northmen yield;
Rule us, as ruled thy father Ring,
    Son of the Shield!

"Be Frithiof regent of thy house
    Till grown art thou:
Yarl Frithiof, Ingborg as thy spouse,
    We give thee now."

"A king's election," Frithiof cried,
    "Is held to-day,
But not a bridal: I my bride
    Choose my own way.

"To Balder's grove now I must speed,
    For earnest speech
Prepared, my Nornes, full long delayed,
    Are waiting each.

"Tidings to those shield-maids by me
    There must be told,
Where they, around Time's lofty tree,
    Their dwelling hold.

" Still Balder, golden-haired, doth frown
In anger sore ;
He took my bride, and he alone
Can her restore."

Then with a kiss saluted he
The new king's brow,
And slowly o'er the heath they see
Him silent go.

XXIII.

FRITHIOF BESIDE HIS FATHER'S GRAVE.

" FAIR shines the sun, and from its rays of glory,
  From bough to bough the gentle glitter leaps ;
From heaven darts the glance of Odin hoary,
  In dew-drops bright, as over ocean's deeps ;
Like blood on mighty Balder's altar gory,
  In purple all the mountain-tops it steeps.
But soon the earth shall disappear in night,
Soon, 'neath the wave, sink down the shield of light.

" Yet first must I behold each spot so dear,
  Through which, a joyous child, so oft I sped ;
Round the same spring the self-same flowers appear,
  In the same wood the self-same birds are bred.
Still dash the waves upon the cliffs severe ;
  Oh ! happy had I never o'er them fled,
The same false tale of glory ever telling
That lured me, restless, from my happy dwelling.

(167)

" I know thee well, O stream ; thy ripples bounded
　　Full often as my swimming form they bore ;
　Valley, I know thee, where, with shade surrounded,
　　A lasting love, unknown to earth, we swore ;
　Ye birch-trees bright, whose bark so oft I wounded
　　With deep-graved runes, ye stand forth as before,
Bearing on silvery stems the forest crown :
All is unchanged, except myself alone.

" Is all unchanged ?   Oh ! where is Framnäs' hall ?
　　Where Balder's temple on the sacred strand ?
　All the dear beauty of my native vale,
　　Marred by the sword, disfigured by the brand,
　Of rage of men and wrath of gods, sad tale
　　To wanderers tells the devastated land.
Ah ! pious wanderer, hither shun to rove,
Where beasts have made their dens in Balder's grove.

" Ay, a betrayer stalks through life untiring,
　　The gloomy Nidhögg from the gloomy waste ;
　He shuns the Asa-light, the proud aspiring,
　　Written on flashing sword and dauntless crest.
　He maketh us to yield to his desiring,
　　Dark fiend, he revels in rage unrepressed,
And when a temple flames, delightingly
Clappeth his coal-black hands in furious glee.

" Hath no atonement place in Valhall's hall ?
　　Can nought, bright Balder, soothe thine angry mood?
Men can be pacified whose comrades fall :
　　The lofty gods we reconcile with blood ;
And thou art called the mildest of them all :
　　Speak, and I offer gladly all my good.
Thy temple's burning Frithiof never willed ;
Take this disgrace from his once stainless shield.

" Remove the weighty burden of my woes,
　　Drive from my soul the ghosts of gloomy thoughts ;
Let life-long grief and sorrow interpose
　　To wipe away the guilt a moment wrought.
I should not quail, though Thor were of my foes,
　　And ghastly Hela fearless should be sought ;
But thee, great spirit, shining bright and clear,—
Thee, and the vengeance sent by thee, I fear.

" Here rests my father—if a hero sleeps ;
　　Thither whence none returneth he is gone ;
Mead-quaffing in the starry tent, he keeps
　　Glad revel, joyous in his armor's tone ;
Guest of the gods ! glance downwards thro' the deep,
　　Thine offspring calls thee, Thorsten, Viking's son ;
With spells of deep enchantment come not I ;
How shall I Balder please ? is all my cry.
8

" Giveth the grave no answer ? For a sword,
 Angantyr, long-departed, spake not he ?
Tirfing was good, yet little worth such word ;
 I ask for more—no sword contenteth me ;
Battle can weapons plentiful afford.
 Bring thou, O father, peace from heaven with thee ?
Be thou the pleader of my sorrowing prayer ;
No noble heart can Balder's anger bear.

" No sound, my father ? Hark ! the ocean sings,
 In its sweet voice—oh ! speak a word to me ;
The storm-wind flies, hang thee upon its wings,
 And whisper to me as its swift gusts flee ;
The western sky hangs full of golden rings,
 Let one of thy dear counsel herald be.
What ! For thy son's despair no sign, no breath ?
How poor, my father, is the sleep of death ! "

The day sank down, with evening breezes singing
 To man their lullaby so soft and mild ;
The sunset, rosy-cheeked, its glories flinging
 In purple radiance, girt the heavenly shield ;
Round azure heights and verdant valleys clinging,
 Valhalla's semblance all the circle filled :
When sudden o'er the western billows came
A lovely vision, weft of gold and flame.

O'er Balder's bounds the gentle Hägring hovers,
    (For so we call it, though in Valhall' bright
More sweetly named,) and floating downwards, covers
    Green hill and dale in coronet of light,
Spreading around, as far as eye discovers,
    Unfancied splendor, wondrous to the sight ;
And as at length it down to earth descends,
A temple, on the temple's site, it stands.

Vision of Breidablick !   Towards heaven rearing
    Their height, the walls with silver seem to vie ;
The mighty pillars of dark steel appearing ;
    A single jewel forms the altar high ;
Forth hangs the dome, as if by spirits bearing,
    Starry and beauteous, like the winter sky,
And there, in azure garb and golden-crowned,
The gods of Valhall' seem to sit enthroned.

Within the portal stands each noble Norne,
    Together bearing Fate's Rune-written shield ;
Three roses gathered in a single urn,
    Solemn, but wondrous beautiful and mild.
Urd towards the ruined shrine doth silent turn,
    Skuld to the vision of the new revealed ;
And scarce is wond'ring Frithiof conscious grown,
From glad amaze, ere all again is flown.

" Oh ! I have comprehended, maidens fair !
 My father, thou hast shown a sign of good :
The ruined temple I again shall rear,
 Superb upon the rock where once it stood.
Oh ! happy thus, no longer to despair,
 Of peaceful deeds atoning insult rude.
Again in hope the outcast wretch may live,
Since Balder bright doth pardon and forgive.

" I hail you, stars, as gently ye arise !
 Your silent course again with joy I see.
Hail, northern lights, around the arching skies !
 A temple's flames full oft ye've seemed to me ;
Grow green, dear grave, again ; again arise
 Forth from the waves, thou wondrous melody !
Here, slumbering on my shield, I'll dream in peace,
Of man forgiven, and immortal's grace."

XXIV.

RECONCILIATION.

COMPLETED now was Balder's temple. Round about
Stood not, as once, a willow-pale ; of iron wrought,
With golden knob on every rail, was set the fence
Of Balder's grove, and like a steel-clad armament,
With halberts bright and golden helmets, stood it forth,
And sentinelled the sanctuary now renewed.
Of mighty stones enormous was its circuit built,
With wondrous art together joined, a giant work,
For endless ages raised, like Upsal's lofty shrine,—
Where in an earthly form the North Valhalla sees.
Proud stood it on the lofty cliff, and mirrored forth
Its towering summit in the ocean's shining wave ;
And far around it, like a splendid belt of bloom,
Spread Balder's valley fair, with all its rustling groves,
With all its songs of joyous birds, a home of peace :
High stood its copper-bolted portals, and within
Two pillars tall upon their mighty shoulder-blades

Upheld the lofty dome, which hung forth beautiful
Above the temple, like a giant shield of gold.
Farther within, great Balder's altar stood, outhewn
From one huge block of Northern marble, and around
A sculptured serpent cast its coils, deep-graved with
    Runes
In wisest words from Vala and from Havamal.
But in the wall above a space was found adorned
With stars of gold upon a ground of blue ; and there
The god of Goodness' silver image was, as fair
As silver moonshine throned upon the azure sky,
So seemed the temple.—Now in pairs there en-
    tered in
Twelve temple-maidens fair, in silver raiment clad,
With roses blooming on their cheeks, and roses, too,
Within their guileless hearts : before the image dread
They danced around the altar newly consecrate,
As spring-time's breezes dance above the rivulets,
As forest elves dance lightly o'er the tall-grown grass,
While still the morning dew lies glittering around.
And 'midst their dancing sang they, too, an holy song,
Of Balder, the all-pious ; how beloved was he
Of all creation : how by Höder's dart he fell ;
How earth, and sea, and sky lamented ;—such a
    song
It seemed as ne'er from out a mortal bosom sprung,
But like a tone from Breidablick, the Bright One's
    hall ;

Like dream of loved one which a lovely maiden
    dreams,
When in the peace of silent night deep pipes the
    quail,
And moonlight beameth o'er the birch-woods of the
    North.—
Delighted Frithiof, leaning on his sword, beheld
The dance ; and many a scene of childhood's glad-
    ness sped
Before his sense, a merry race and innocent.
With eyes of heavenly blue, and lovely heads, adorned
With curling locks of floating gold, they nodded forth
A loving greeting to the comrade of their youth.
Then like a bloody shadow sank his Viking's life,
With all its battles fierce, its past adventures wild,
Down into darkness, and unto himself he seemed
To stand, a flower-decked Bauta-stone, upon its grave.
And ever as the song swelled high, his spirit rose
From lowly vales of earth on high to Valaskjalf ;
And earthly rage and earthly hate were melted down,
As Winter's icy mail from breast of Earth dissolves,
When shines the sun of spring ; a flood of gentle
    peace,
Of glad delight, his noble bosom overflowed.
It seemed as if the heart of Nature he could feel
To throb with his ; as if with gladness he could clasp
The whole Heimskringla in his loving arms, and
    make

In sight of heaven a holy truce with earth.
Then entered Balder's sacrificing priest the shrine,
Not young and fair as Balder, but a towering form,
With heavenly mildness in his noble countenance,
And downward to his belt his beard of silver flowed.
Then new-felt reverence filled Frithiof's haughty
    soul ;
And lowly bent the eagle-wings upon his helm
Before the sage, who thus in words of friendship
    spake :

"Son Frithiof, welcome hither : I have watched for
    thee :
For youthful vigor wanders glad round earth and
    sea,
Like Berserk pale, who biteth furiously the shield,
But wearily and thoughtful wanders home at last.
Full oft enough to Jotunheim sped mighty Thor ;
Yet spite of magic belt, and spite of gloves of steel,
Utgårda-Loke sitteth ever on his throne ;
To no might Evil, mighty in itself, will yield.
And profitless is piety unmatched with power,—
'Tis like the sunbeam playing over Ægir's breast,—
A changing glow that sinks and swells with every
    wave
Without a settled depth, unstable, insecure.
But power wanting piety devours itself,

Like buried battle-blade ; it is life's wild carouse,
Where o'er the beaker's brim oblivious Haeger
    soars,
And when the drinker wakes, he blushes for his
    deed.
All vigor is of earth, from corpse of Ymer sprung ;
Forth from its veins the stormy waste of waters
    flows,
And all its sinews are of brazen metal forged.
But void, and desolate, and fruitless, it must lie,
Till Piety, like heavenly sunlight, shines thereon.
Then grass grows green, and spreads a carpet
    flower-weft ;
Then lift the trees their crowns, then gleams the
    golden fruit,
And man and beast draw life from mother Nature's
    breast ;
So is it, too, with Asker's offspring.   Odin hath
Two weights within the balance of each mortal life,
Each counterpoising each when fairly stands the
    scale,
And they are named, the Love of Heaven, the
    Might of Earth.
Full strong is Thor, O youth, when close he clasps
    around
His mighty loins the magic belt, and strikes amain ;
And wise is Odin, when on Urda's silver wave
He gazeth down, and round about his ravens fly,
    8*

And bring him tidings up from earth to lofty heaven ;
Yet pale grew both, and half was quenched the gleam
    that decked
Their royal crowns, when Balder, pious Balder, fell ;
The clasping link was he in Valhall's wreath of gods.
Then yellow grew the splendor of the tree of Time ;
And Nidhögg gnawed upon its root ; then loose were
    set
The powers of agéd Night ; the Midgard serpent
    raised
To heaven its coils' envenoméd, and Fenris howled ;
From Muspelheim the sword of Surtur lightened
    forth.
Since then, where'er the eye can turn, the battle
    fierce
Throughout creation rageth on ; in Valhall crows
The cock gold-crested, and the red one crows to
    war,
On earth and deep beneath the earth. Yet erst was
    peace,
Not only in the hall of gods, but here on earth :
In breast of men, as well as breast of lofty gods.
For whatsoever happens here hath happened, too,
More wondrously above ; and so the life of men
Is but an image slight of Valhall ; heaven's light
Reflected down on Saga's rune-engraven shield ;
And every heart of man its Balder hath. Thou'st
    known a time

When peace within thy bosom dwelt, and gladsome
    sped
Thy life, in heavenly calm, like dream of sweet-voiced
    bird,
When winds of summer night rock gently to and fro
His greenwood nest, and bend the heads of slumber-
    ing flowers,
Then Balder still was dwelling in thy stainless soul,
Thou Asen-born, thou wandering type of Valhall
    pure !
For children still doth Balder live, ana Hela yields
Her booty back as oft as child of man is born.
But in each heart of man, with Balder, groweth up
His brother, Höder, blind, the child of Night ; for Ill,
Like young of bears, is sightless born, and dark-
    ness is
His covering, while Balder clothes himself in light.
But ever-busy Loke tempts unceasingly,
Misleads the blind one's murderous hand, and guides
    the spear
Against the heart of Balder, Valhall's best beloved.
Then Hate awakeneth ; for prey Might springeth up ;
Like hungry wolf, o'er hill and dale, the greedy sword
Doth prowl, and dragons swim upon the bloody
    waves ;
And shadow-like, of power bereft, doth Piety
By Pallid Hela sit, as dead, amongst the dead ;
And low in ashes Balder's holy temple lies ;

And thus the life of gods above foreshadoweth
The life of men below, and both together are
Allfather's silent thoughts, which never know a
    change.
What hath been, what shall be, doth Vala's deep
    song tell,—
A song at once the lullaby, the dirge of Time.
Therewith in unison, Heimskringla's tale is told,
And thence may each man hear his own heart's his-
    tory ;
And Vala asks of thee : 'Canst understand thine
    own ?'

"Atonement seekest thou.—Oh ! know'st thou
    what it is ?
Gaze in mine eyes—oh! Frithiof, gaze, and turn
    not pale ;
Atonement bears on earth no other name than
    Death ;
All time is but a measure of eternity ;
All life,—an emanation from Allfather's throne ;
Atonement,—thither purified to hie thee home.
The lofty gods themselves are fallen. Ragnarök
Is their atoning day appointed ; day of blood
On Vigrid's hundred leagues of plain ; there must
    they fall,
But never unavenged ; since Evil then must die

Eternally, and fallen Good arise on high,
From flames of earth to loftier being purified.
'Tis true, the rayless wreaths of pale-grown stars
Shall fall from heaven above, and Earth in ocean
    sink ;
But, joyously, another new-born Earth shall raise,
From ocean forth, its fairer, flow'r-adornéd head ;
And wandering stars renewed, with sweet, benignant
    beam,
Above the new creation take their silent course.
Once more shall Balder, then, upon the grassy hills,
Rule god's regenerate and purified mankind.
The Rune-writ golden tablets, lost so long ago
In early dawn of time, shall then again be found
On Ida's plains, by Valhall's reconciléd race.
Thus, death is but an ordeal for fallen good,
And its atonement, birth into a better life ;
So, purified, it flieth thither, whence it came,
Rejoicing guileless, as a child on parent's knees.
Alas ! that all that noblest is must lie beyond
The grave—the grassy gate of heaven ; and all that
    dwells
Beneath the stars be base, by evil maculate.——
Yet some atonement still may here on earth be
    found,
A partial, gentle prelude to the perfect one ;
Like hand of minstrel straying o'er his harp, before,
With skilful fingers, he awake the voice of song ;

By gentle proof he tries the tuned accord, and then
His bold hand striketh mightily the golden strings,
From out the grave invoking memories of yore,
And Valhall's brightness flasheth from his trancéd
    eyes.
So earth the shadow seems of heaven above ; and
    like
The entrance court to Balder's temple in the skies ;
And sacrifice to gods is made ; by purple rein
The steed is led in golden trappings to their shrines.
Therein a figure, deep of meaning, lies ; for blood
Must be the morning-dawn of all atonement-days.
But neither type nor figure can themselves atone ;
Thy deeds of evil done can none make good for
    thee.
Atonement for the dead is in Allfather's breast ;
Atonement for the living in each living heart.
One sacrifice I know, in heaven above more dear
Than smoke of slaughtered oxen : 'tis to offer up
Thine own heart's angry rage, thine own revenge.
Canst thou not blunt the edge of passion, and for-
    give ?
Then, Frithiof, nought hast thou to do in Balder's
    house :
And vain must be the temple which thou here hast
    reared.
With stones thou canst not please the god ; with
    peace alone,

On earth below, and heaven above, forgiveness
    dwells.
Be reconciléd to thy foe and to thyself,
And so shalt thou be reconciled to Balder bright.
'Tis said a Balder southward dwelt, the Virgin's
    son ;
Allfather sent him forth to make the purport known
Of writings dark till now upon the shield of Fate.
His rallying-cry was Peace, and Love his shining
    sword,
And Innocence sat, dove-like, on his silver helm.
He lived the holy life he taught ; forgiving, died ;
And, far away, 'neath spreading palms, his grave is
    made.
They say, his teaching spreadeth on from vale to
    vale,
And melteth hardened hearts, and layeth hand in
    hand,
Erecting strifeless empires on the peaceful earth.
I know not well the lore he taught, and yet, me-
    thinks,
At times, in better hours, its thoughts have come to
    me ;
At times such thoughts fill all men's hearts as well as
    mine.
The day will come, I know, when he shall gently
    wave
His snowy, dove-like pinions o'er the northern hills.

But, ere that day, the North shall pass from us
      away,
And oak-trees murmur over our forgotten graves.
Oh ! generations blessed, privileged to quaff
The beaming cup of new-born light, I bid ye hail.
Rejoice ! rejoice ! when it shall drive each cloud
      away,
That hung its misty veil before the sun of life ;
Yet shun to scorn our race, which, ever constant,
      .   sought
With unaverted gaze its heavenly beams to view :
Allfather, though but one, hath many messengers.

" Thou hatest Bele's sons.   And wherefore hatest
      thou ?
Because with thee, a yeoman's son, they did not will
To match their sister, who is sprung from Seming's
      blood,
The son of Odin, and because their pedigree
Ascendeth up to Valhall's throne ; and they are
      proud.
But thou wilt answer : ' Birth is chance, and not de-
      sert.'
No man, believe me, youth, of his deserts is proud ;
'Tis but his better fortune ; and the best of all
Is, after all, a gift of Heaven.   Art thou not proud
Of all thy valiant deeds, of all thy matchless might ?

And was that might conferred by thee ?   Did Thor
    not knit
The sinews of thine arm as firm as branching oak ?
Is thine high heart no gift of God's, that boundeth
    glad
Within that citadel, thine arching breast ?   And is
That lightning not of heaven that flasheth in thine
    eyes ?
The lofty Nornes already by thy cradle sang
Of glorious life to come ; therein thy merit is
No greater than a king's son's for his royal birth.
Condemn not others' pride, lest thine, too, be con-
    demned.
For now is Helge fallen."   " How !" cried Frithiof
    loud,
" King Helge fallen !   Where, and when ?"   " Thou
    knowest well
That while thy temple thou wast building, he was
    gone
To war in Finnish highlands.   On a lonely cliff
An ancient shrine he found, of Jumala the seat,
For many a year gone by closed up and desolate ;
But still an agéd, wondrous image of the god
Above the gate remained, and nodded to its fall ;
But no man dared to venture near, for it was said
Amongst the Finns, from sire to son, whoever first
Within that temple trod should Jumala behold.
This Helge heard, and blindly scaled, in bitter rage,

The lonely steps that led to the detested god,
Desiring to destroy the shrine. He reached the top ;
The key was rusted, fast within the portal locked.
He laid his hands upon the post ; in rage he shook
The rotten portals ; all at once, with frightful crash,
The idol's image fell, and crushed beneath its weight
The heaven-born Helge.—Thus he Jumala beheld.
A messenger this night hath brought the tidings
    home ;
Alone now sitteth Halfdan on King Bele's throne.
Give him thine hand ; to heaven thine anger sacri-
    fice ;
This off'ring Balder doth demand, and I, his priest,
As proof that now thou mockest not the peaceful
    god.
If thou refuse, in vain this temple hast thou reared,
And vainly have I spoken."

                              Halfdan entered now
Across the copper threshold, and, with doubtful
    glance,
He stood aloof from Frithiof feared, and held his
    peace.
Then Frithiof snatched the breastplate-hater from
    his side,
Against the altar set his golden-orbéd shield,
And all unarmed, advancing, stood before his foe.
" In such a strife as this," he spake in kindly voice,

" He noblest is who offers first a friendly hand."
King Halfdan blushed, and off his glove of steel he
    drew :
Those hands so long apart were joined again
In vig'rous clasp, as firm as rock's deep base.
The graybeard then the heavy ban revoked that lay
Upon the Varg-i-Veum, excommunicate.
And sudden, while the words he spake, came Ing-
    borg in,
In bridal garb,—in ermine mantle,—maidens fair
Behind her following, as heavenly stars the Moon.
With tears within her beauteous eyes she fell upon
Her brother Halfdan's breast ; but, deeply moved,
    he laid
His sister, well beloved, on Frithiof's faithful heart.
And Ingborg, over Balder's altar, gave her hand
To him, her childhood's friend, her heart's delight.

NOTES TO THE AMERICAN EDITION.

———•———

PAGE 1.—" FRITHIOF AND INGEBORG." In this Canto, the last couplet of each stanza, in the original, has invariably feminine rhymes.

Page 3, line 16.—A more literal translation of this stanza seems preferable :

> But childhood's days full fleetly glide :
> There stands a stripling in his pride,
> With haughty eye that hopeth, pleadeth,—
> There stands a maid whose bosom buddeth !

Page 19, line 6.—" *Hans sjelf en lefvande saga* "—himself a living *tradition*.

Page 31.—" FRITHIOF'S WOOING." Here, again, in the original, the rhymes of the last couplet are feminine.

Page 45.—" FRITHIOF'S JOY." " Frithiof's *Bliss* " is a more correct translation.

Page 124.—" VIKINGABALK." The Viking-Code.

Page 158.—" RING'S DRAPA."   The effect of the Saga-
measure depends on its alliteration.   This necessary feature
Mr. Blackley has neglected in his translation.   As a specimen of its character, I give the first stanza :

> Sits in the sepulchre,
> Son of the heroes,
> Battle-blade by him.
> Buckler on arm :
> Neigheth his stallion
> Standing within it,
> Stamping with gold-hoof
> The gate of the grave.

ALPHABETICAL GLOSSARY AND NOTES

———◆———

AEGIR. The ocean-god. Daughters of Aegir, the waves.

AESIR. The twelve highest gods, namely, Odin, Thor, Njörd, Frey, Tyr, Heimdall, Bragi, Vidar, Vali, Ullur, Hænur, and Forsete, with their progeny.

ALFADER (All-Father). The highest title of Odin.

ANGURVADEL (Flood of anguish). The name of Frithiof's sword.

ASEN. The gods. Asa-sons, or Asen-sons ; a name generally given to Scandinavian kings, who were supposed to trace descent from the gods themselves.

ASKER, or ASK. The first man.

ASGARD. The city of the gods.

ASTRILD. The god of Love.

* *The Translator is indebted for the extracts from the "Prose Edda," in this Glossary, to Mr. I. A. Blackwell's translation of that production, contained in his new edition of Mallet's "Northern Antiquities," 1847 ; and has also profited largely by remarks in other parts of his work, which he takes the present opportunity of acknowledging.*

(191)

BALDER. The god of Light, typified by the Sun. The following account of him is taken from the "Prose Edda," c. 22 : " The second son of Odin is Balder, and it may be truly said of him that he is the best, and that all the race of man are loud in his praise. So fair and dazzling is he in form and features, that rays of light seem to issue from him. Balder is the wisest, the mildest, the most eloquent of all the Aesir ; yet, such is his nature, that the judgment he has pronounced cannot be altered. He dwells in the heavenly mansion called Breidablik, into which nothing unclean can enter." Balder, or Day, was, at the instigation of Loki, god of Mischief, slain by the blind god, Hödur, or Darkness.

BALE-FIRE. A beacon-fire. That referred to in the text, No. XIII, was the fire kindled on Midsummer's Eve, in honor of Balder, the god of Light, whose symbol, the Sun, at that period seemed to reach its highest power. It may be remarked, in passing, that ignorance of the history and meaning of the word Bale, or Bal, has very far diverted its original sense in our use of its compound, *baleful*, which, properly signifying fiery, full of light, or flame, is used in English in the sense of *malignant*. The heathen custom of lighting bale-fires or bonfires on Midsummer's Eve is still continued in parts of Northern Germany, Scotland, and Ireland, though the practice is generally supposed to be intended in honor of the coming festival of St. John the Baptist, which falls on Midsummer Day.

BAUTA-STONE. A memorial raised over fallen warriors, and formed generally of a block of unhewn stone, projecting several feet out of the ground. The Bauta-stone differed from the Rune-stone in being uninscribed, the memorial Rune-stone bearing, on the contrary, an inscription in the form of a serpent, surmounted by the sign of a hammer, the emblem of Thor, god of War.

BERSERKIR. A. class of mythical heroes imbued with an implacable frenzy for war. Hence a proverbial expression for any warrior of unusually ferocious disposition.

BIFROST. The rainbow. It may be interesting to remark the coincidence between the Eddaic account of the rainbow, and Sir David Brewster's theory of *three* primitive colors. The following is from the " Prose Edda," chap. XIII : " ' I must now ask,' said Gangler, ' which is the path leading from earth to heaven ? ' ' That is a senseless question,' replied Har, with a smile of derision : ' hast thou not been told that the gods made a bridge from earth to heaven, and called it Bifrost ? Thou must surely have seen it ; but, perhaps, thou callest it the rainbow. *It is of three hues*, and is constructed with more art than any other work,' " &c.

BJÖRN. *Lit.*, a bear. The name of Frithiof's comrade. Hence the play on words, page 82 :

> " Björn, come to the rudder ;
> Hold it tight as *bear's hug*."

BLŒTAND. *Angl.*, blue-toothed.

BLOOD-EAGLE (to tear the). A custom of putting to death an enemy under circumstances of peculiar atrocity. The ceremony consisted in carving on the back of the prostrate foe the figure of an eagle, and so separating the ribs from the back-bone. In the text, Björn promises to perform such vengeance on Frithiof's slayer, should his chief fall.

BRAGE. The god of Poetry and Song.

BREIDABLIK. Broad-gleaming, latifulgent. Balder's palace in the heavens.

BUDKAFLE. The bidding-staff. A wand about a foot in

9

length, inscribed with certain characters of authority; and which, sent from house to house with great dispatch, formed a summons for the assembly of the whole nation to deliberate on public matters of moment. This custom bears a strong analogy to the sending round of the fiery cross in the Scotch Highlands on the like occasions. The practice in Scandinavia, as well as in Scotland, is minutely described by Sir Walter Scott, in the Notes to the "Lady of the Lake," Canto III, stanza 1.

DAYLIGHT OF DWARFS.   From the idea that the Earth was supported by four dwarfs, North, South, East, and West (see page 10, line 6), came the belief in the existence of a subterranean race of dwarfs, who were supposed to be lighted by the veins of gold in the bowels of the earth.

DELLING.   Twilight, dawn.   Son of Delling—Dagr, Day. See "Prose Edda," c. 10: "Nott (Night) espoused Delling, of the Aesir race, and their son was Day, a child light and beauteous like his father. Then All father took Night, and Day, her son, and gave them two horses and two cars, and set them up in the heavens, that they might drive successively round the world. Night rides first on her horse, called Hrimfaxi (Rimy, or frosty-maned), who every morning, as he ends his course, bedews the earth with the foam which falls from his bit. The horse made use of by Day is named Skinfaxi (shining-maned), from whose mane light is shed over the earth and the heavens."

DISARSAL.   The hall of goddesses.

DRAGON'S BED.   The dragon Fafner, guardian of the Nibelungen treasure, was fabled to lie upon it.   Hence, gold was said to be gathered from the dragon's bed.

DRAPA.   A triumphal song in honor of departed heroes,

sung, for the most part, at the "grave-feast," which all heirs, on succeeding to their fathers, were bound to hold. When sung by Brage himself, the god of Song (as in No. XXI), it signifies a hymn of welcome rather than a dirge.

EFJESUND. In the Orkneys, of which Angantyr was Yarl.

EINHERIER. *Angl.,* chosen heroes. All who, dying a violent death, were admitted to the joys of Valhalla.

ERIKSGATE. The solemn progress which the Scandinavian kings were accustomed to make through their whole realm after their coronation.

FAFNER. The dragon set to watch over the golden treasure, but conquered by Sigurd, the Siegfried of the Nibelungenlied.

FAFNER'S-BANE. Destroyer of Fafner. A surname given to Sigurd for the exploit referred to above.

FOLKVANG. The palace of Freya in the heavens, the supposed habitation of virtuous and beautiful women after death.

FORSETE, or FORSETI. The god of Justice.

FREY. "One of the most celebrated of the gods. He presides over rain and sunshine, and all the fruits of the earth ; and should be invoked in order to obtain good harvests, and also for peace."—*Prose Edda,* c. 24.

FREYA. The goddess of Love. "The most propitious of the goddesses ; her abode in heaven is called Fólkváng. To whatever field of battle she rides, she asserts her right to one-half of the slain, leaving the rest to Odin."—*Prose Edda,* c. 24.

FRIGGA. The spouse of Odin, and mother of the Aesir.

GANDVIK. The White Sea.

GEIRSODD. *Angl.*, spear-death. In contradistinction to
straw-death, *i. e.* death from disease or age. Suicide,
practised by aged warriors to insure their admission to
Valhalla, where none dying a natural death were admitted.

GERDA. The most beautiful of women ; spouse of Frey.

GLITNIR. The palace of Forsete in the heavens.

HÄGRING. The Fata Morgana. A well-known, though
rarely witnessed phenomenon, said to be occasionally
presented on the Norwegian coast.

HAM and HEYD. Two storm-demons, or weather-sprites.

HAVAMAL. *Angl.*, the lay of the sublime. An Eddaic
poem, containing a number of precepts said to have
been given by Odin to mankind. Many of those given
by Bele and Thorsten to their sons in the text are actu-
ally adopted by Tegnér from the Havamal, as may be
seen by comparing, for instance, page 12, stanzas 5, 6,
with the following extracts from the ancient work :
" Praise the fineness of an ended day ; a woman when
she is buried ; a sword when you have tried it ; the
ice when you have crosssd it ; and liquor after it is
drunk."—" Trust not the words which a woman utters,
for their hearts have been made like the wheel that
turns."—" Trust not to ice of one day's freezing ; neither to the sleeping serpent," &c. &c.

HEIMSKRINGLA. The universe.

HELA, or HEL. Goddess of Death ; ruler of Niffelhem,
the abode of all who died of disease or old age.

HILDUR. The goddess of War.

HÖDUR. The god of Darkness. See *Balder.*

HOLMGANG. A single combat. So called from being very
frequently decided upon a lonely island (Holm), without witnesses, and, of course, *à l'outrance.*

IDUNA. The spouse of Bragi, god of Song. She is keeper

of the apples of immortality, by which the youth of the gods is continually renewed.

IDA'S PLAINS. *Orig.*, Ida-vallen. *Lit.*, the valley of confluence. The dwelling of the gods after the destruction of the universe.

JERNHÖS. The iron-headed.

JUMALA. A deity worshipped by the Finns. The term has passed into a name for the Almighty Being, and (as the Countess von Imhoff remarks) our Lord is named in the Finnish, Jumala Poyke.

JÖTENHEIM, or JUTENHEIM. The giant's home, or region of the giants.

LOFN (sometimes LOFNA, but less correctly). The presiding deity of Matrimony. The term (from which our word *love* is derived) signifies unchangeable affection.

LOKI. The god of Evil and Mischief; descended from the race of the giants.

MIDGARD SERPENT. The great serpent said to encompass the whole earth.

MIDNIGHT SUN. This expression (No. XIII, stanza 1) may sound strange to many readers, unless they bear in mind that in parts of Sweden and Norway the sun does not sink below the horizon at all at the period (Midsummer) referred to in the text, but remains visible from high ground through the whole night.

MIMER. The owner of the well of wit and wisdom, at the root of Yggdrassil (the ash-tree, symbolical, according to Finn Magnusen, of universal nature). Mimer, always drinking of his well, was imbued with the highest wisdom.

MORVEN. The north of Scotland.

MUSPEL-HEIM. The region of Muspel; the world of flame;

thus described in the "Prose Edda," c. 4 : "In the
south is the world Muspel. It is a world too luminous
and glowing to be entered by any not its natives. He
who sitteth on its borders to guard it is called Surtur.
In his hand he beareth a flaming falchion, and at the
end of the world shall issue forth to combat, shall vanquish all the gods, and consume the universe with
fire."

MUSPEL'S SONS. Flames.

NANNA. The spouse of Balder, who died with grief at her
husband's death.

NASTRAND. The strand of the dead.

NIDHÖGG. The down-hewer, or down-gnawer. A dragon,
said continually to gnaw at the root of the ash, Yggdrassil.

NIFFELHEM. The land of shadows.

NORNES. The Fates, or Destinies, three in number. Their
dwelling was beneath the ash Yggdrassil, by the fountain of Mimer. See Völuspá, stanza 17 : "Thence
come the much-knowing maidens, three, from that
fountain which is beneath the tree. One is called Urd
(the Past) ; another, Verdandi (the Present) ; and the
third, Skuld (the Future). They engrave the Runic
tablets ; they determine the lives of the sons of men ;
they lay down laws ; they settle destinies, &c.

NORRĀNA TUNGA. The old Norse language.

ODIN. The most mighty of all the gods.

ODIN'S BIRDS. "Two ravens sit on Odin's shoulders, and
whisper in his ear the tidings and events they have
heard and witnessed. They are called Hugin (Thought)
and Munin (Memory). He sends them out at dawn of
day to fly over the whole world, and they return at eve,
towards meal-time. Hence it is that Odin knows so

many things, and is called Hrafnagud (the raven's
god)."—*Prose Edda*, c. 38. Hence ravens, generally,
are called the birds of Odin.

OEDUR. The spouse of Freya. He "left his wife, to travel
into very remote countries. Since that time Freya
continually weeps, and her tears are drops of pure
gold. She has a great variety of names; for, having
gone over many countries in search of her husband,
each people gave her a different name."—*Prose Edda*,
c. 35.

PILLARS OF SHAME. These were the Niding-posts, or me-
morials on which the name of any one guilty of cow-
ardice or other disgraceful conduct was inscribed.

RAGNARöK. *Lit.*, the twilight of the gods. The destruction of the universe, a desolation minutely foreshadowed
in the "Prose Edda." This period is referred to in
No. XXIV, where the references sufficiently explain
themselves.

RAN, or RANA. The goddess of the sea.

ROTA. One of the Valkyrien, which see.

RUNES. The characters of the Scandinavian alphabet, sixteen in number. To these letters many marvellous
properties were assigned; they were used sometimes
as charms against misfortune, sometimes against ene-
mies, sometimes to secure victory. They were said to
have been invented by Odin himself, as well for the
common purposes of life as for magic.

RUNENBALK. A staff, graven with Runes, and supposed
to have some magic efficacy.

SAGA. The goddess of History.

SEMING. A son of Odin.

SIGURD.   The Siegfried of the Nibelungenlied, conqueror of the dragon Fafner.

SKALD.   The title of the northern bards.

SKOAL.   A toast in honor of any person or thing.

SKINFAXE.   The horse of Day.   See *Delling*.

SKULD.   See *Norne*.

SLEIPNER.   The steed of Odin, having eight legs, and excelling all horses ever possessed by gods or men.

SOLUNDAR-OE.   The Hebrides.

SÖQUABACK.   The mansion of Saga in the heavens.

SURTUR.   The god of Fire.   See *Muspel-heim*.

THOR.   The god of War, wielder of thunder.   He is represented always afoot, and armed with a short-shafted hammer.

THRUDVANG.   The dwelling of Thor.

TING.   The general assembly of the Northmen, which all capable of bearing arms were bound to attend on occasions requiring deliberation or action.   The word is still used, Volks-Thing being applied to the Swedish assembly.

TIRFING.   The sword of a warrior named Angantyr, which was buried with its owner.   His daughter Hervor, however, desiring to gain the weapon, caused her dead sire to remonstrate against the proceeding.

UTGARDA-LOKI.   See *Loki*.   Thus called from his dwelling, Utgard, said to be at the utmost limit of the universe.

URDA.   See *Norne*.

VALA.   A spaewife or prophetess.

VALASKIALF.   Odin's dwelling in heaven.

VALHALL, VALHALLA.   The paradise of warriors.

VALKYRIA, VALKYRIE.   Choosers of the slain.   " Prose
Edda," c. 36 : " There are, besides, a great many other
goddesses, whose duty it is to serve in Valhalla ; to
bear in the drink, and take care of the drinking-horns,
&c.   They are called Valkyrior.   Odin sends them to
every field of battle, to make choice of those who are
to be slain, and to sway the victory," &c.

VARG-I-VEUM.   Outlawed.   Under the Ban.